MW01640286

Angels &
Promises
of Silver Falls
VOLUME 2 OF THE SILVER FALLS SERIES

Rebecca Woods

Sweetwater Books
An Imprint of Cedar Fort, Inc.
Springville, Utah

ISBN 13: 978-1-59955-997-1

Published by Sweetwater Books, an imprint of Cedar Fort, Inc., 2373 W. 700 S., Springville, UT 84663
Distributed by Cedar Fort, Inc., www.cedarfort.com

Photography of Hannah and the Oregon coastline by Savannah Woods.

Cover design by Rebecca Jensen
Cover design © 2012 by Lyle Mortimer
Edited and typeset by Michelle Stoll

Printed in the United States of America

10 9 8 7 6 5 4 3 2 1

Printed on acid-free paper

I lovingly dedicate this book to my beautiful daughter-in-law, Carolina. Thank you for all that you do and for being such a natural and awesome part of our family.

Contents

Chapter One

Hannah Layne
April 1906

It was tradition among the local families to name their roosters after a favorite chicken dish, as it was frequently their fate. So it was, with the approaching dawn, that Fricassee ruffled his feathers against the cold, strutted outside, and took his place atop David Harrison's tallest fence post. Letting out a robust crow, he challenged all others in the vicinity to the usual morning contest of vocal virility.

The sun, not yet fully up in Silver Falls, was evident enough only to cast muted hues of rose and lavender over the fog-wrapped farms. Cacciatore, balancing himself on the ridge pole of Andrew Layne's clapboard home, soon stretched forth his neck, crowing his reply, to which Drumstick answered from John's house beyond in the distance. Not a minute later, Cordon Bleu, refusing to be outdone, hauled himself out of the hay, flew to a window of Nathan's barn, and let out his own terrific crow.

As if on cue, the songbirds began to twitter and sing among the dew-laden foliage of the maples. Flitting in and out of the dripping leaves, they ruffled their feathers in an attempt at drying themselves and mustering some warmth. The early morning in Silver Falls had arrived, a dense fog gathering in the lower hollows as the brook drifted along beyond the barn, past the house, and on its way toward the ocean cliffs.

The frigid air, on the verge of a rare vernal frost, pressed in on the windows and walls of the gray stone house across the bubbling brook. Inside, the fires had long ago succumbed to mere ashes, allowing the temperatures to drop there as well.

Knitting her brows, Hannah shivered in the cold as she struggled through a dark and disturbing dream. In the recesses of her unconscious, the snow fell in large white flakes all around her, forming a thick blanket over the graves, old and new alike, with the exception of one. Her shawl falling loosely around her shoulders, she ran her hand over the frozen ground, refusing to let the storm entomb it further. Her tears coursed down, dropping to the earth and freezing where the snowflakes would have lain.

"Oh, Nathan," she whispered, "please come back to me; don't leave me here."

There was no response from the mound as she continued to brush the surface, running her hands over the earth again and again. She was numb with cold, her fingers white and far beyond feeling. At last, she collapsed over the dirt, allowing herself to be covered as well.

Spotting her from the iron railing, David walked quickly, picking his way through the stones until, at last, he came to his sister's side.

"I thought I'd find you here," he whispered. "Let's go home, Hannah; you can't stay any longer." When she did not answer, he began to pull her from the snow. "Come, Hannah, you will freeze out here; you cannot stay."

Pulling her from the grave and into his arms she began to cry. "He'll be cold, Davy; I can't leave him."

David looked down at the fresh mound of earth. Everyone was ridden with grief, but Hannah was out of her senses with it.

"Come with me, Hannah," he said quietly. "You're frozen through; your hands are like ice. You can stay with us until you're through this."

"No," she cried, leaning back.

"Hannah," David began to shake her, hoping to bring her to her senses. "Hannah," he shook harder as the white flakes began to swirl around her, fogging everything from her vision.

"Hannah, love, wake up; you're dreaming. Wake up."

Nathan was gently shaking her, trying to rouse her from sleep.

Slowly, she opened her eyes and tried to make sense of where she was. The April dawn was slowly creeping into the room as she tried to focus her eyes on the concerned face of her husband, the grief of the dream still gripping her heart.

"You were dreaming, love."

Settling into his arms, feeling his warmth and strength surround her, she tried to let the ache ease from her soul.

"It was so real," she whispered. "I've never dreamt anything so real before."

Nathan kissed her forehead and settled back into the pillows, succumbing once again to his sleepiness. "It's all right now, Hannah. What was the dream about?"

Snuggling further against him, trying to convince herself that he was real and the other merely a nightmare, she ventured her thoughts.

"I dreamt you died; I was crazy with grief. Davy was trying to pull me away from your grave, and I was so cold. The snow kept covering it and I felt I had to keep it clear or you'd never come back to me."

"You are cold," he smiled. "You must have gotten your arms out of the blankets. It's much colder than usual this morning. I should have put more wood on the fire last night; it feels like winter in here rather than spring."

"It was so real."

"Yes, Hannah, but it was only a dream, and hardly a fitting one for our anniversary, I might add. Remember we are going to look at horses today. I found out Joe Henrie also has a few choice mares he's thinking of selling."

Trying to pull herself from the lingering melancholy, she attempted to change her thoughts.

"It's been your life's dream. Will you really do it this year? Oh, promise me you will, Nathan. The farm work is making you old before your time. Every year you plant so much, far more than we need, and then you nearly collapse at the harvest in the heat from the work of it all."

He could hardly argue; all she had said was accurate, and then some. "I suppose this year would be as good as any to start pasture instead."

She was quiet after that. In the drama of her sleep, she had completely forgotten the day, but it was their anniversary—April fifth. Four happy years ago today they had been married. She let her mind drift back over the past to the events of that day and the few prior to it as they rode the train to Colorado.

Nathan had played along the entire time, not once venturing onto the topic of marriage. As often as she attempted to bring it up, he would change the subject, until she feared she would have to ask him herself. But it was just like him, wanting the moment to be perfect, and being laden with bank cares on a stuffy, overcrowded train certainly wasn't what he'd had in mind.

Aunt Nanette was nearly in shock when she answered the door, but graciously invited them in and visited with Hannah while he took care of his business at the bank. She had been in the midst of making her own preparations to leave for Boulder, their daughter Elena needing help in her confinement since the birth of her baby. Adam had planned to go for a few days as well, and they were to leave that night.

Unknown to Hannah, while she was busy visiting over tea and cookies, Nathan had traded the gold and secured the money home to George, all within a couple of hours. Stopping by the bakery on the way back, he brought a pack of cream puffs for all, as well as a new cheerfulness and relief to his own spirits.

Adam allowed them to stay in his home, and it had been that night, in front of the crackling fire, that he had finally, *finally* asked her again and, oh, it had been romantic! She smiled at the thought. Despite her frustrations on the train, Nathan knew how to be romantic when he wanted.

She had hoped to get married right away, the very next day, before anything more could thwart their plans. He thought they should wait . . . though amidst the kisses and promises of forever love, his argument wasn't long lived. By the following day, they had obtained a marriage license and wedding clothes.

It was a very small ceremony, but when Nathan lifted her veil and looked into her eyes, nothing could replace the joy that she both saw and felt. She didn't think that life could ever be happier than that single moment had been. Smiling again, she snuggled closer.

"Do you remember when we got married?"

"Hmm," he murmured in his sleepiness.

It was hardly a definable answer, but she understood that in the interim of her thoughts he had fallen back to sleep. It was about as close to "yes" as she would hear for the moment.

"You wanted to wait until July," she laughed.

A smile tugged at the corners of his mouth. "I didn't really want to wait at all; I just wanted to see your reaction."

"I wish we would have waited, at least until we got back."

"Why? I thought you liked it there, the cabin and the mountains."

Hannah smiled again at the memory. "I did, that part was perfect. It was only the wedding. Who did we have to share it with?"

"Caleb was there, and Marian."

"Yes, I suppose that was all right, but I wish your parents could have been there, and your family, and my family. Susannah would have been in heaven over it."

This time Nathan laughed. "Yes, she was a little sore at missing out on it, wasn't she? But I'm glad we married there and didn't wait. Ten years was plenty long enough for me."

"Did you hear that Uncle Adam is coming out again for the dance festival?"

"No, with the whole family?" he asked.

"Yes."

"When did you hear that?"

"They wrote to your parents last week to let them know."

"That will make their third year in a row, but it's months off yet. I wonder why they wrote so early."

Hannah just shrugged. "Do you remember the first time we ever did those dances, Nathan? I should have married you then, the first time you wanted. Surely we would have a family by now."

"Don't torture yourself, Hannah. We wouldn't have been who we are today had we married back then." Nathan smiled wryly. "Besides seventeen was much too young; I'd have never figured out how to provide for you."

"Seventeen? You were well over twenty-two."

"You said the first time I wanted, and I wasn't even quite seventeen. I remember it to the day; you had come over to borrow something for Laurel. You were so beautiful; I was nearly heartbroken when you said you couldn't stay. I wanted to follow you home, convince Laurel that she really didn't need you so badly after all, then take you home and keep you. It was then that I realized the only way that could ever be was if I married you, and nothing ever sounded better."

"And here I thought we were friends," she smiled.

"I thought so too, up until that day, but the thought of marrying you was all it took. I knew I loved you and I knew I would never be completely happy until you were mine."

"So, now that I'm 'yours,'" she ventured once again, "do you suppose we'll ever have more of a family than just us?"

Nathan was quiet for some time. "Four years? I don't know. It is in God's hands, Hannah, and if he chooses to bless us that way we will count ourselves fortunate. Otherwise, I suppose we're better off remembering that there are greater challenges in this world and be thankful that our family is as complete as it is." Gathering her further into his arms he added, "I'm thankful I have you, Hannah, my love. Children or no children, as much as I want them, I'm thankful that you're my wife."

She smiled again, snuggling into his shoulder. He was so warm, and the love which filled her now was complete and in such contrast to the dream. After all, she thought, trying to cast it completely aside, it was only a dream.

Chapter Two

A QUESTION OF COURAGE
AUGUST 1906

An air of anticipation filled the crowded room as the festival participants began moving into their places. Standing willowy tall and mature for her fifteen years, her long dark hair falling nearly to her waist, Janette, the youngest daughter of Adam Layne, had arrived from Colorado that very morning. She excitedly made her way up the steps to the cultural arts building with her best, long-distance friend, Susannah Harrison. As they came into the room, the girls paused to check the list on the table.

Kelly had mentioned that as soon as she had a better idea of who was planning to attend she would arrange partners for them both and would have the arrangements listed on the roll at the door. Presently, Susannah heaved a rather large sigh of disappointment; her partner was to be Larry Moore. Larry was younger than she by nearly two years and had the reputation of never being able to remember the steps.

Janette, finding her name on the list, asked. "Who is Gabriel Taylor?"

"Only the handsomest boy in town," Susannah answered. "Why?"

"He's my partner."

"That's not fair, Janette. Why do I have to dance with Larry and you get Gabriel?"

"I don't know. Who's Larry?"

"The boy over by the window, with the freckles. He's only twelve and has two left feet."

"Oh. Well, tell me more about this Gabriel fellow. How old is he?"

"He must be seventeen. I don't know him well, but Josie Dane will be green with envy when she finds out he's your partner. She's had a crush on him for years."

"Josie Dane? Isn't that the girl we locked in the outhouse at the picnic last summer?"

Susie giggled. "Well, she's the one you locked in the outhouse, and though it was over a year ago she's still mad at you for it, I'm sure. She can carry a terrific grudge. Maybe we'd better trade partners just to be safe."

"No thanks," Janette smiled. "I'll count it all as divinely appointed. Where is he?"

"I don't see him."

"All right, class, let's begin." Kelly clapped her hands to call them all to order. "Come in girls; Susannah, you're with Larry." Larry smiled grandly at his partner while she did her best to manage a polite smile in return. "Janette, come to this spot. Gabriel will be back in a minute."

Janette did as she was told, and then watched as each boy took his partner's hand and raised it to the starting position. "Better to have a child for a partner than no partner at all," she was thinking to herself, when all at once she heard a voice behind her.

"Hi, you must be Janette."

She turned to see a most exquisitely handsome young man. Trying to find words to say hello, she instead found herself most inconveniently rendered speechless.

"I'm Gabriel; I believe we're partners for the festival. Do you know the dances well?"

Janette managed a nod before they were off and into the thick of the final practice before the performance. She found it hard not to stare at him while they danced; he was so beautiful with his finely chiseled features, black hair, and deep blue eyes. She marveled at his eyes most of all; they were magnificent! Each time she looked at him, he gazed back so intently that she felt as though they'd had a blending of souls, making it all rather difficult to concentrate on her steps.

The evening's practice passed as though it were a mere moment in time, and before she knew it, Gabriel was bowing gallantly to her at the conclusion of the last number.

"Thank you, Janette," he began in his melodious voice. "You're a wonderful dancer. I'll look forward to seeing you tomorrow night."

She managed a flushed smile as he left, then turned to find Susie. Poor Susie! Larry was competing for her attentions with two other boys who appeared even younger than he.

"Susie, dear, we have to hurry or we'll be late," she declared.

Grabbing her hand, Janette pulled Susannah from the circle of boys, while each of them gazed back at her in surprised disappointment.

Once outside, Susannah laughed. "Thank you, Janette, but late for what?"

Janette only put a finger to her lips as they passed out of the crowd and started on their lengthy walk home. Once safely out of earshot, she whispered her excitement.

"Oh, Susie, what a dream! Please, tell me everything, absolutely everything that you know about him."

"There's not a whole lot really; he's so much older than me. I only know that Josie is in love with him and threatens us with the evil eye if she catches anyone so much as looking his direction."

"Ah, Josie Dane," Janette repeated thoughtfully. "She's awfully territorial, isn't she? Does he like her too?"

"I don't think so. She's around him a lot, but I don't think it is by any of his own choosing. When he excuses himself from a crowd, she follows him to the next."

"Oh, Susie, did you see how he looked at me? I felt like the Queen of England dancing with him. He is so dashing."

Susannah laughed again. "Well, the festival is tomorrow night; at least you'll get to see him once more before you leave."

"Only once?" she moaned. "How sad to think of leaving; I want to stay forever."

"At least you have a week."

They walked the rest of the way home with only occasional conversation while Janette sighed continuously, quite lost in her thoughts and the anticipation of the following night.

It was still early morning when Hannah drove down the Harrison lane with Dolly and the buggy. She was coming to pick up Susannah, who had promised to help with the preparations. There was much to be cleaned and put in order before that night, and Kelly would need all the help she could get. Hannah was a little surprised when Janette showed up at the door as well, but counted her blessings at the addition. They could certainly use the extra help.

Pulling into the Mayers' lane, the enormous barn looming before them, they all felt a certain thrill for the event which was only hours away. Once inside, however, the scene that met their eyes was a little more sobering to the spirit.

The Mayers were supposed to have the building emptied out, yet each year proved to be a larger mess to clean than the last. As Hannah and the girls stood in the cool shade of the first floor and scanned their surroundings, they observed tools and debris strewn everywhere. Mountains of lumber ends lay intermixed with piles of sawdust, dirt, and dust-encrusted spider webs. The familiar other "leftovers" one might expect from a working barn were there as well. Thankfully, most of the festival would be happening upstairs in the massive hayloft.

Hannah sighed at the task and mentally tried to picture the effect of hanging quilts to block the view of all but the stairs to the top. It would certainly save a lot of time.

"Why is it that we always save this to the very last minute?" she wondered aloud.

"Well, it was supposed to be clean, wasn't it?" Susie asked.

"Yes, it was," John answered, coming into the barn at that moment. "I'm pretty sure it is the only real reason the Mayers let the Society use the barn at all. It does guarantee a thorough cleaning at least once a year."

Hannah smiled at that. "Well, I say that this year we forgo cleaning most of the first level and instead hang quilts to block the view. The stairs and railing do need a good sweep though," she observed.

Eventually, they all rolled up their sleeves, took a deep breath, and dug in, working mostly on the upper level to transform the building for the evening's event. They had been raking, sweeping, and cleaning for about two hours when Gabriel walked in.

"Hey, Mrs. Layne," he called from the door. "The 'boss' said you're in charge; what should I do first?"

Hannah, thankful to see more male help arrive, immediately put him to task moving some of the heavier items. He worked for several minutes before finally spying Janette. Casually, he made his way over to be in her general vicinity.

"Hi," he offered quietly. "I didn't know you were going to be here."

Janette tried to remain calm, though her heart was beating wildly. "I didn't know you were going to be here either. How did you come to be drafted for such a job?"

Gabriel smiled, looking deeply into her eyes. "Sheer luck, I guess."

Janette swallowed hard and glanced over at Susannah, who could hear every word and was fighting off a torrent of giggles. She was trying to think of something to say in return when Hannah called him off to help with something else. Then he was gone, off to the first floor of the barn for the next several hours. In the meantime, Kelly had shown up with yet another crew, which started on the decorations for the old building.

The Mayers were one of the oldest families in the district, having arrived in the early days, before the town of Silver Falls had even been established. Josiah Mayer had been a young boy then, when his grandfather and nine sons banded together to settle several large tracts of land. By law, they could only claim as many acres as they could reasonably farm, but by joining forces, they could accomplish much more than any one person could manage on their own. They first set up a sawmill and then built the great barn in the center of those lands, one large enough to meet all of their needs. After that, they began spreading out to build their houses. As the years wore on and his grandfather eventually passed away, it was the eldest, Josiah's father, who inherited the land with the enormous barn. When his father died, it fell to Josiah, and while it handily met all of his farming needs, it was large enough that it never went fully utilized. In the meantime, it stood as an effective status symbol and occasional community outlet.

The folk dance festivals had been held here on a regular basis for many years, with Kelly in charge of them from the beginning. It was routine, time after time, getting all the decorations where they needed to be; it was only the ever-increasing dirt and debris that required all the extra labor.

By midday, the barn appeared ready for the event. Long garlands, colorful festive wreaths, and a very many lanterns bedecked the rafters and walls, while elegantly draped tables and chairs filled the areas not reserved for the dancers. Kelly, surveying the preparations, finally pronounced it complete, and the Laynes were all preparing to leave just as Gabriel came back into the room.

"Are either of you bringing Janette tonight?" he asked quietly.

"No, Gabe," Hannah answered. "I believe she's coming with her parents. Why do you ask?"

"I was wondering if I might pick her up."

The two women looked at each other in surprise. "You'll have to ask her father," Hannah answered.

Gabriel grimaced at that and backed down completely. Instead he smiled and shrugged. "Well then, I suppose it must be time to get home and clean the rest of the Mayers' barn off of my person." He then turned and left, giving one last, obvious glance toward the beautiful Janette.

The Laynes, having all arrived a little early, were gathered around the refreshment table, catching up on the latest news between the widely separated families, which their earlier tasks of the day had prohibited. Janette and Susannah stood with the group, milling around and waiting for a little more excitement to show.

They had spent far too much time through the afternoon, primping and priming each other to the pinnacle of visual perfection, to be wasting such efforts on mere family. While Susie looked very lovely indeed, Janette was the one who captured the greatest effect of their efforts. Her dress fit to her young figure as though tailor-made, her cheeks were ablush, her lips deep red, and her eyes sparkling with excitement. Her hair glistened down her back, decorated by the pink and gray ribbons of a dried flower garland that rested at the crown of her head. The family was laughing at some witty remark of John's when Gabriel Taylor came through the door, followed by Josie Dane.

"Do you suppose he brought Josie?" Janette whispered.

"Not likely; I thought I saw her waiting outside."

Scanning the room, Gabriel finally landed his sights at the refreshment table and headed in that direction, with Josie still in tow. He waved to Janette and winked just as someone pulled him from his course, thwarting him from his destination. It was then that Josie and Janette met each other's gaze.

Josie's eyes flew wide open in shock and anger as she closed in on her victim. "You!" she whispered in tones of complete contempt. "Who told you that you could come?"

"Good evening, Josie," Janette began amiably.

"You have no right to be here," she touted back. "Why don't you go home where you belong?" Josie was careful to keep her words quiet, though they rang with certain and definite threat.

"I really like your dress," Janette retorted. "Tell me, what made you choose that one over something in fashion?"

Josie fumed. "You ought to be locked up, Janette Layne, and never allowed out."

"I suppose it's an idea, but I'm not as overly fond of outhouses as you are."

Susannah erupted in laughter as Josie shot her a death glare. Finally, she spoke, in between giggles. "Oh look, here comes Gabriel."

Josie's eyes narrowed while she shook a finger at Janette. "Don't you even entertain the idea of speaking to him," she threatened. "He's mine!"

"Oh, you wish," Susannah countered as Gabriel came up and took her friend by the hand.

"Janette," he said, pulling her off and away from the crowd, leaving Josie to gape.

Eventually, gathering her wits, Josie Dane turned to Susie. "Susannah Harrison, you tell that brazen man-snatcher that this is war."

Susie looked off across the room long enough to see that Janette and Gabriel were safely away and already engaged in conversation. "You'll have to tell her yourself."

"Kelly says you're visiting from Colorado," Gabriel began in an attempt at some casual conversation. "How long will you be staying?"

"One more week."

Knitting his brows he ventured casually. "Do you have a steady beau back home?"

Janette nearly laughed. "Not at the present."

Truthfully, at fifteen, she had never had a beau of any kind, steady or otherwise, but this was not something she wanted to admit just now. Instead, she was feeling quite relieved at coming up with such a smooth answer. Her heart had felt in her throat and her stomach filled with butterflies since she had first spotted him.

"What about you?" she managed. "Who are the women in your life?"

"My mother and three sisters," he smiled.

"And Josie?" she pursued.

Gabriel looked confused. "Do you mean Josie Dane? Why, Janette, she is a mere child who follows me like a puppy. I've never entertained the idea of regarding her past that."

Janette felt suddenly sorry for her earlier rude remarks. Josie was obviously an underdog already, and she shouldn't have added to her misery. Before she could dwell on it longer, however, the musicians began playing the cue for the dancers to take their places and the festival to begin.

Spinning her around in a sweeping motion, Gabriel took her into his arms and positioned them both for the first dance. Squaring his shoulders in confident stature, they awaited the music while Janette marveled at how wholly distinguished and refined he appeared. It was like this the entire evening as they danced. All the while, he held her heart captive with his eyes, keeping his sights quite steadily fastened on her.

Gabriel's thoughts were preoccupied with, perhaps, a wee bit more than the folk dances as he watched her closely, admiring the softness of her skin and the curves of her slender figure. As the last formal dance of the festival came around, he drew her very close to him, much closer than the dance called for and, attempting to whisper in her ear, he let his lips brush across her cheek.

"Janette, can I take you home tonight, please?"

Thrilled at the request and more than a little embarrassed at the fact that she was not old enough to speak for herself, Janette tried her very best to remain calm.

"I'll ask my dad," she answered.

In the next minute the band began to play, and once again Gabriel held her close to him, very close, as if to keep the request foremost in her thoughts while they danced and twirled across the floor.

The applause was thunderous as that divine, final number came to a close, and Janette wasn't at all sure whether she had walked or floated across the room after that. All she remembered was that he had given her hand a squeeze and let her go. In the next moment, she stood before her parents in a state of euphoria and blissfully stated her desires.

Adam Layne's brows knit as the question was broached. "Janette," he began in mildly irritated tones, "I'll not let you go home with any man who hasn't the courage enough to ask me himself. The answer is no."

"But Papa, please. We'll only be here a week and I was really hoping . . ."

"Janette, I said no, and no is what I meant."

She knew it would be useless to plead further. When Adam Layne spoke in that tone, his word was final. Scarcely able to contain her disappoint, she returned to Gabriel, who had been waiting on the other side of the room, and tried to explain in a way that might not discourage him completely.

"I'll be staying at my Uncle Andrew Layne's house," she offered at last. "Maybe another day would work out better."

"Can I take you driving then, later in the week?" he asked, still obviously hopeful.

Janette hesitated over the question. She dearly wanted to go with him and couldn't understand for even a moment what the big fuss about "courage" was. Finally, she leaned close and whispered back. "There's nothing I'd love more, Gabriel, but you'll have to ask my father."

A reticent look came over his face as he glanced across the barn toward Adam Layne. Appearing deep in thought for several moments, he let out a long sigh and, at last, took her hand in his arm, heading instead for the refreshment table.

"Let's get some punch."

The festival was its usual thrilling success, providing the community with more entertainment than could be found anywhere west of the coastal range. Each year, the crowds grew larger until there was hardly standing room and talk ensued of making the performance run for multiple nights in order to accommodate the numbers. Most of those present agreed that these rare cheery affairs passed far too quickly, not happening often enough. Eventually, however, it was time to leave, before the full moon set and the travelers were left without such means to light their way home.

Most of the Laynes stayed on afterward to defrock the loft of its gala glamour, getting everything loaded back into the wagons and taken home to be stored for another year. Gabriel stayed as well, lingering as near to Janette as he could manage while staying as far away from her father's terse gaze as possible. The night could not have lasted long enough for either of them.

Finally it was time to go. As the horse trotted placidly down the road, Adam looked over in the moonlight to see his daughter in a full pouting session.

"What seems to be the problem, my little Janette?"

Maintaining her defiant silence, she turned her head to look out the other way across the fields.

Her mother, noticing it as well, offered her thoughts. "My guess would be it has something to do with that handsome young man she was dancing with. What was his name, my love?"

"His name is Gabriel Taylor; he's perfectly elegant, and I can't understand what the big deal is about courage. How can you know if he has courage or not just because I asked you instead of him?" She was obviously still furious over the entire issue.

Adam Layne looked out across the wide expanse of the night as he measured his thoughts and words carefully.

"You're a beautiful girl, Janette," he explained, "and you will always be my baby. I would give my life to protect you. It will be hard enough ever handing you over to another man, and until one comes along that can show he has enough courage to stand up for you and protect you as I would, then you needn't waste your breath on the fellow. Anyone who was half a man wouldn't send a young girl off to ask her father if she could drive home with someone he's never met. I know what I'm talking about, little girl. Now, let's not spend another minute being angry over it."

As bruised as she felt earlier over the affair, she had to acknowledge to herself that she couldn't maintain a lasting grudge over someone who loved her as much as that. Furthermore, while she waited the rest of the week with bated breath, Gabriel never did show to make his request.

"Maybe," she admitted reluctantly in her disappointment, "Papa might be right."

Chapter Three

QUEST FOR GOLD
AUGUST 1906

The lamp shone dimly through the small room, casting shadows against the log walls, as the kerosene smoke mixed with the dank smell of whiskey, grease, and stale tobacco. Two middle-aged men sat at the table, one of them under siege of verbal abuse as he rolled his eyes and mocked his accuser whenever her back was turned. The old woman circled the table and then stopped to shake a finger at her son.

"Bartholomew Baines, I did not raise you to be no treasure seeker. You gotta do somethin' with your life instead of constantly comin' cryin' home to your Ma for more money. Make somethin' of yourself. Get a job; settle down. You ain't gonna find that gold any no how and you wasted your life lookin' for it. Now look at you; you got nothin' to show for yourself but a drunkard and a bum with no money, no wife, no nothing."

"I don't need no stupid wife," he snarled. "Besides, Ma, I have found it and if you'll . . ."

"Don't you go lyin' to me," she snapped back. "I've had all I'm gonna take from you and your whiskey wanderin' ways; you'll not use me up like you did your pa! No sir; you can beg your livin' elsewhere 'til you're ready to shape up. Now, I'm leavin', but I'll be back, and I don't want to find you here when I come, you hear me?" she announced as she started for the door. "Good for nothin' bum," she muttered angrily, slamming the door behind her.

"I think you must've caught her on a bad day," his brother offered casually.

"Nah, Ted," he drawled, "it's actually one of the nicest things I ever heard her say to me."

Both men gave a knowing smile before the younger continued. "Maybe if you came home more often than to ask her for money she might like you a little more. Why do you go on searchin' for such a hopeless cause anyway? You know you'll never find it."

"No?" the man replied. Reaching deep into his pocket and pulling out the contents, he separated two small items from the rest and tossed them across the table. "What do you think they call these, moron; peanuts?"

Ted fingered the small golden objects with great interest. "They's ingots, ain't they?"

"I'll say they are," his brother snapped, grabbing them back. "I found the ship, or at least part of it, and the chest."

Ted's eyes opened wide in excitement. "You found the gold?"

"No, I found the chest, but it was mostly empty. There were maybe a couple dozen ingots in and around it and a few more buried in the sand. I collected eighty-one in all, but someone else got there first, and I intend to find out who."

"How? It could've been scores of years ago."

"Not likely. The wear on the broken slats wasn't anywhere near as worn as the rest. I'd guess it couldn't have been more than ten or twenty years at the most. And was that water ever cold! I nearly froze to death trying to get what I did. I say it would be much easier trying to find out who has it and get it that way."

"But who do you suppose has it? It could be anyone."

"Not anyone, stupid; someone very rich. I traced several ingots down to a general store in a town called Silver Falls, which happens to be the closest town to the wreck. The owner said it came to him 'anonymously' several years back. He couldn't remember exactly, but thought it was ten, maybe fifteen years ago. He said that most people believed it came from a man named Mayer. I checked into the Mayer guy and he was rich all right, one of the richest around, but so was his father. Most likely it wasn't him."

Bartholomew turned the gold over and over in his fingers. "There were a few others, someone named Langston who moved from the east eight years ago, and another man named Price who came to the area about twelve years ago. Langston came too late to consider, but this Price fellow is a possibility. Then there's a family by the name of Layne. They were farmers, several brothers of them, but they somehow got up enough money between them to start a bank. They're regarded as generous and well-off by the others in the town, but the numbers don't figure. One of the brothers is a doctor, but young, too young to have found the treasure. Three of his older brothers run the bank, Mark, George, and Nathan. The dad still farms with another of the brothers."

"Do you think it's them?"

"Mark would be my first guess of the lot. He lives in town in a big ol' fancy house and walks around like he owns the place. George, I found, lives out on the edge of town under comfortable but much more humble conditions. I had a tough time locating Nathan. He rarely ever showed up to the bank the whole time I was there, but someone said he lived in the country and farmed a large spread."

"I guess you'd cross him off the list then."

"That's what I thought, at first." He was contemplatively fingering the ingots. "Then I started asking myself questions. If he was so intent on farming, why be involved in the bank at all? It doesn't figure. When I asked the store keeper about the bank he said that Nathan was the president."

"Maybe all the brothers found the gold," Ted offered.

"Maybe, but I don't think so. I'd say it would have to be between Mark and Nathan, or possibly both. Still, it doesn't add up at all to my thinking. How can a very young man, and a farmer at that, be founder of a bank? No, I think Nathan is the one we're looking for. He probably has it hidden out someplace on his farm."

"So what you gonna do?"

"I still need to find his farm, but I need money to pursue it."

"Well, you got all them ingots; ain't they worth a pretty picture?"

"Yeah, so I sell them and every other Joe who's been searching for that treasure traces them down just the way I did. Not hardly, Ted; I need cash."

His brother paused thoughtfully. "I got some; it ain't a lot, but it's some. I'll pitch in if you share the treasure."

The older brother smiled slyly. "Sure, Ted. Here, have an ingot for collateral."

"When will we go?"

"Soon; it's a long ways off. It will take weeks to get there, and the weather'll only get worse before it gets better. We need time to do more snooping before we can make a move."

"What'll you do if he won't hand it over?"

Bartholomew smiled banefully. "Kill him. It's a hard thing for a dead man to keep his fortune."

Chapter Four

THANKSGIVING
NOVEMBER 1906

"Nathan, would you fire up the other stove? There isn't enough room for things in here."

It was Thanksgiving Day, and the Laynes were combining their efforts in taking a turn to host the traditional feast for their families. It seemed that, in reality, they hosted it more often than not; for each time one of the other wives had a new baby or sick children, Hannah was the one they would ask to cover for them. Being that her energies weren't taken up with little ones, it only made sense to their thinking. After all, Mother and Dad were getting older now and the other wives didn't feel it proper to put the burden of so much work on them.

Sarah Layne often wondered why they never thought to ask each other and instead assumed that Hannah should take it on. She also wondered at how Hannah rarely saw anything wrong with it, but hosted them time after time. Either way, this year it really was their scheduled turn, regardless of any other turns taken or missed, and in the early morning hours the preparations were well under way.

Nathan surveyed the counters heavily laden with rows of dark orange tubers. "Why so many yams?"

"Because it's a favorite and there will be so many people this time."

"I guess we must be up to fifteen by now," he mumbled a little absently.

Hannah smiled to herself; he obviously hadn't counted them for a while. "No, actually I think we are closer to thirty-two."

"Thirty-two! Are we also hosting for the bank employees?"

She smiled as she worked. "No, just your family. Mark and Carolyn plus their children are nine. George's family is five. John and Kelly and their children are seven, that's twenty-one right there. Then Peter and your parents make twenty-four, plus Caleb and his family are here from Colorado."

"But that's only thirty," he announced, taking a seat near her in the kitchen, trying to absorb the numbers. "You said thirty-two."

Hannah stopped in her scrubbing and peeling for a moment, wondering at how sleepy he must still be. Giving him a kiss, she summed up the discrepancy.

"Then there is the Nathan Layne family," she reminded him, "and we are two."

"Ah yes," he said, putting his hand around her waist. "I guess I've always had a tendency to miss the obvious, haven't I?" He sat a little longer as the idea sank in. "Only two," he mumbled. "Hannah, love, we've been up since four o'clock, the turkey is all stuffed and cooking and the sun won't be up for at least another hour. Let's go back to bed and catch up on a little rest. Surely, the yams can wait a while."

"Not a chance. There are still the pies to make and I want the yams all ready by then."

"Pies? Isn't anyone else contributing to this meal?"

"Your mother is doing all the bread and rolls, Marian is bringing the corn, Carolyn has the potatoes, and Janae is making creamed peas."

"What about Kelly?"

"Kelly just had her baby and is still recovering."

"So let me get this straight. We're doing the turkey, stuffing, gravy, yams, cranberry preserves, and the pies? Do I dare ask how many?"

"A minimum of eight. You know your brothers and pie, Nathan."

"I know myself and pie," he mumbled quietly. "All right, love, you win. What's next?"

"For now, I need to get these yams cut and layered; they can cook in the other stove when it's time, and then I'll start on the pies. Everyone is due here at three o'clock."

Working diligently through the rest of the morning and into the afternoon, cooking, cleaning, and setting up tables and benches, they tried staying ahead of all that needed to be done. As the clock chimed three, Nathan was at the door welcoming his parents in. Caleb and his family arrived a very few minutes after that.

"Where is everyone?" Marian wondered aloud, surveying the room.

Nathan pulled out his watch. "I predict John at three thirty, George at three thirty-five, and Mark absolutely no earlier than ten after four."

Hannah had to stifle a laugh. They were all notoriously late, pretty much in that order, and he probably wouldn't be too far off.

"Where's Peter anyway?"

"Someone was sick," Sarah responded. "He said he'd be along as soon as he could."

At length everyone did arrive, John and George, both, at three thirty and Mark with his family at four fifteen. Nathan tried to start seating for the meal as soon as possible, owing to the idea that nineteen hungry children under the age of twelve might more easily be contained while seated under their parent's supervision.

Presently, though the babies were being held, the rest of the children that had any mobility at all were running amok and squealing through the house. Chasing each other up and down the stairs, they flopped on the feather beds, slammed doors, turned on faucets, pounded the piano, pumped the treadle, and someone had just pulled the chain on the toilet for the tenth-plus time in the last half hour.

Hannah wondered at the philosophy of the times, something about "children being seen but not heard." Apparently, it didn't apply here. Eventually, everyone was seated and Grandpa Layne took over as the grandchildren reluctantly quieted down.

"Well this is a sight," he declared, standing and surveying the crowd of thirty people who held the title of being his posterity. "Before we say grace, we'll let each one mention what they are thankful for this year, after which I will offer our prayer."

It was a common enough occurrence, which tradition they had carried through each Thanksgiving Day from Nathan's earliest memories. However, with the ever-growing numbers of children, the food seemed to get a little colder each time. As they started around the table, the parents claimed thanks for such blessings as health, shelter, safety, and family, while the children generally thought more along the lines of pies, peppermint sticks, spiders, snakes, and so forth.

Nathan was thankful for their bountiful harvest that year, and Hannah, who happened to be seated in the order that came last of all, struggled a little. She had thought of several things, but being thirty-second in line, they had all been mentioned and it was tradition not to repeat. After a few seconds, Caleb blurted a suggestion.

"I know, Hannah, you can be thankful that you are free from the cares and worries of children."

A general flutter of laughter went around the table as most of the care-worn parents in the group nodded their approval of Caleb's humor. It was, after all, only a joke. But Hannah was weary and worn. It had been enough to prepare for the group and to longingly observe each of the families bring their little ones in. Now, to gracefully choke back the sting from Caleb's remark took most of her courage. Presently, she felt Nathan take her hand under the table and hold it firmly between both of his.

"I guess," she began, steadying her voice, "that I am thankful to have such a fine husband."

She tried her best to hide the hurt, but Nathan heard it and Sarah Layne heard it and Andrew Layne thought he heard it. Which, perhaps, was why, after the long list of blessings for which he had given thanks in his prayer, Andrew broke from tradition and added a request, that "their gracious hosts might be blessed with the noble desires of their hearts."

As the "amen" was uttered, Nathan began casually deflecting attention to the other side of the table.

"Mark, you have a new tie, don't you?" he asked when they began passing around the food. Mark acknowledged that he did and while all else were admiring it, Nathan took a quick survey of their meal. "I see we have forgotten the napkins. Hannah, I'll help you get them."

He hadn't needed to look at her to know she would be fighting a tide of sorrow, and so ushered her out of the room and into the kitchen. They said nothing for a while; there was really nothing to say. No one meant to be hurtful or thoughtless, but as she gathered the napkins, he caught her hand.

"Hannah, my love, it will all work out," he whispered quietly, before returning to the crowd.

The atmosphere was quite different after dinner, as the children, being so full of Thanksgiving turkey, yams, and pie, milled around quietly or went out to the stable to see Dolly's new foal. Most of the men sat around the fire to visit, while the women seemed to naturally drift back to the kitchen, dishing up and organizing what little left-overs there were. There seemed to be less every year.

"Hannah, you've done so much already," Sarah announced, trying to steer her out of the kitchen. "Why don't you take a few minutes outside and enjoy the weather. It's a beautiful day."

It was a rare, dry day for November, and she found it difficult to resist, especially after Sarah had guided her to the back door and opened it, giving her a friendly shove in the direction of the sunshine. Starting outside, she soon noticed Peter wandering a little aimlessly down the lane.

"Peter," she called, "wait up."

Peter stopped and turned, abiding the request as she approached and took his arm. Slowly, they began walking down the drive, golden leaves drifting down all around them, adding to the carpet of yellow already under their feet. Hannah smiled at the beauty.

"Do you have to leave already?" she asked, noticing that he had his sights set on heading back to town. "It's Thanksgiving; surely, they don't expect doctors to work the entire day."

Peter seemed almost depressed. "I might as well; I'm not doing any good here."

"Doing good?" she questioned. "It is wonderful merely to have you home. What's the matter, Pete? You look so glum."

He hesitated in his thoughts, looking off over the hills. "Dad isn't well," he finally whispered. "He's been showing all sorts of signs of heart failure, but he won't listen to me in the least. He says he's fine and waves me off as though I were no one."

"Your dad loves you, Peter; maybe he's afraid. I'm certain it's the doctor he is dismissing and not his son."

Peter laughed a little to himself. "We got into an argument over that very thing earlier today."

"Really; what happened?"

"Dad told me to drop it once and for all. He said 'doctor or not,' he expected me to still honor my father. I told him it was difficult to honor someone that wasn't going to be around."

"Ooh," Hannah winced, "that was a testy response. What did he say to that?"

Peter paused again, looking down at her. "He didn't say anything for a long time. We simply stood there, out in the barn, locked in an angry staring contest. Finally, he softened and told me that if I lived a good and honorable life, I would bring honor to his name whether in this life or out. Maybe Nathan could talk to him," he mused as he looked back to the farm. "They've always gotten on best."

"What would you want him to say?"

"If Dad would just slow down, I'm sure he could add more time. He keeps insisting that he'll go when it's time and not sooner or later."

"Does Mother know about this?"

Peter shrugged. "Not about this morning; we were outside in the barn. She's heard me mention it before, though. That was one of the reasons Dad told me to drop it. He said it was only worrying her, and he wanted to enjoy whatever time he had left. I don't know what else to do."

"I don't know that there is anything you can do. I'll talk to Nathan and let him know. He and Dad always have had a way about them, haven't they?" she smiled.

Peter smiled too. "Yeah, they have. Maybe he'll listen to Nathan," he added with a short laugh.

Coming back to the house, they found that the children had made their way inside and were beginning to make such a ruckus that the men in the room were nearly shouting to be heard over the roar. Finally, Mark stood and, with a clearing of his throat, announced that they still had Carolyn's family to visit and they'd best be leaving.

Hannah was ever so slightly grateful, as Mark's children were the loudest and most active of the entire group, generally leading the rest on from one piece of raucous behavior to the next. Mark and Carolyn were nice enough, but even Mrs. Layne, who generally kept her opinions very much to herself, felt that this one set of grandchildren could use "perhaps a touch more discipline."

As the door closed behind them, though the din was still great, the house became instantly more peaceful. Hannah noticed Andrew and watched him closely the rest of the day, though he seemed healthy as ever and was having the time of his life playing with his grandchildren. Surely, Peter had misjudged his condition. Maybe he was feeling overwrought with care from his other patients. Whatever the case, it was obvious there was no crisis for the time being. She would bring it up to Nathan, but not today, not when everyone was so happy and enjoying the pleasantness of the holiday.

The children continued their noisy play for another several hours before the festivities were finally called to an end, the leftovers handed out, and the remaining families carted their respective small fry off to their own houses. This left Nathan and his wife quite alone in their home for a thankfully quiet Thanksgiving night.

Nathan settled into his chair before the fire, rested his feet on the ottoman, and breathed an involuntary sigh as Hannah brought him a cup of warm, spiced cider.

"Hannah, love, are you sure we want children? Some of those here today weren't much better behaved than little beasts."

Hannah gave a sideward glance at her husband and, seeing the exhaustion on his face, couldn't help but smile. Beasts? It might have applied to a few of them.

"Our children will be different," she assured him.

Beyond the stone house in the tranquility of the night, an owl called from a branch in the maples, while the brook bubbled peacefully along toward the waterfall at the beach. Under a blanket of stars that shone over the district of Silver Falls, all was so very quiet outside and in, at last.

Chapter Five

A Strange Visitor
December 1906

Three more weeks passed as the weather turned colder and frost became an almost constant companion of the night. The days were descending to their ebb, while the familiar darkness of winter settled in around four o'clock and remained until after eight each morning.

Late one evening, Hannah sat sewing before the fire and warming her toes, while her husband finished up his evening chores by lantern light in the barn. It had been an extremely cold day, the clouds constantly threatening to shed their contents but never quite committing to do so.

While sitting there, finishing up the last few touches on some gifts, wondering whether or not they might get snow for Christmas, she heard a knock at the door. It nearly startled her out of her seat. They rarely had visitors and almost never at night. Quickly, she rose and went to answer.

"Who is it?"

"A servant of the Lord, ma'am," a man's voice called back just as Nathan came through the back door to the kitchen. Feeling safe in his presence, she opened the front door to be greeted by a very old and ragged man.

"Good evening," he bowed graciously. "I am just passing through and wondered if you might be able to spare a little food."

Nathan joined his wife at the door. “Yes, certainly; come in and warm yourself while we get you something to eat.”

He showed him over to the fire, as Hannah left the room to gather a quick meal.

“Will you be in Silver Falls long?” Nathan asked, while the old gentleman settled into a chair.

“No, son,” he replied; “just passing through. I have work to see to in Albany.”

“Then you have a ways to go. Will you be taking the train?”

The man paused and looked down. “No,” he said at last. “I’ll be on my own two feet. I have no fare for trains.”

Nathan marveled that anyone would attempt to walk such a distance, especially at this time of year, let alone a man as old as this. His shoes were worn and beaten and his jacket frayed. He looked so poor that Nathan wondered when his last proper meal had been. At about this time, Hannah returned with some cider and biscuits.

“The rest is warming on the stove,” she offered, “but this should get you started.”

He thanked her as she left and was trying to be consciously polite, though it was obvious he was voraciously hungry. Nathan excused himself and went into the kitchen, where he was satisfied to find that she had prepared a generous portion. After a few more minutes Hannah returned to the front room with a plate of steaming, nutritious food, which the man, hungry as he was, received with joy.

“Where are you staying the night?” Hannah asked, concerned for the stranger and the cold that was outside, hoping he didn’t have far to go before he reached his next destination.

“Usually see if I can bed down in a barn for the evening while I’m traveling,” he replied.

“In a barn?” she asked, quite in shock. “On a night like this? Why, it is threatening to snow outside.”

“Perhaps you can stay the night here,” Nathan offered. “We have plenty of room.”

The man looked very surprised, before nodding his approval. “I’d be much obliged.”

“Then that’s settled,” he announced. “We’re the Laynes; I’m Nathan and this is my wife, Hannah.”

“Brother John,” the man offered with another nod between bites.

"Do you have family near here?" Hannah asked.

"No, ma'am," he replied.

"Brother John" seemed short on words and long on hunger, so they let him finish his meal without further questions. When he was done, Hannah rose to collect his plate, cup, and utensils.

"Thank you again for the food," he offered most gratefully.

"Well, it's getting late," Nathan concluded. "If you would like a bath, there are clean towels on the shelf in the bathroom."

The man thanked him but declined, so Nathan showed him to his room and saw that he was settled. Almost immediately, he appeared to sink into a profound slumber. It was so very odd.

Later that night, as they slept, Hannah kept dreaming that groups of desperately poor people were coming to their door. She didn't know any of them and felt more than a little apprehensive allowing strangers into the house, but it was cold outside and she couldn't turn them away. She dreamed the same dream all night long, and when she awoke in the morning, though it was still dark, she thought she heard someone say that she would be blessed.

"Nathan, did you say that?" she whispered, though she quickly discovered that he was still asleep.

Surely, it was merely a remnant of her dream. She thought of waking him, but instead got up and began breakfast. With the smell of sizzling bacon filling the house, Nathan woke up soon enough and joined her in the kitchen.

"Good morning, love; you're up early," he offered, running her hair through his hands and kissing her on the cheek.

"I didn't know when that poor, old man would have to leave," she whispered, "and I didn't want to send him away hungry."

"Yes, I was thinking of seeing him onto the train this morning. I don't like the thought of him walking all that way, not in this cold."

"Maybe he likes to walk," she smiled.

"Perhaps," Nathan laughed, "but we can still offer. I'd like to do something about his shoes too, if I can. I wonder if Carroll's has any in stock."

"I wonder when he needs to leave."

They didn't have to wait long to find out, for the smell of bacon, eggs, and griddlecakes had roused their guest from sleep as well.

As they all sat around the table, "Brother John," as he liked to call himself, began to speak.

"Mr. Layne, you've been most generous. I don't have much with which to repay your kindness, but before I leave today, I wonder if I might, as a servant of the Lord, leave a prayer and a blessing on your home."

The words quickened Hannah's heart, though she was immediately disappointed to hear Nathan thank him but decline the offer. She had been quiet through the previous conversation, but at this point she burst out.

"No, Nathan! Please, let him."

Embarrassed by her own emphatic words and the return surprised looks of the men around the table, she lowered her eyes and said no more.

"Very well, Hannah." Then turning to the old man, he added. "We'd like to offer you train fare to your destination, if you will accept it. I'll be going into town a little after breakfast."

Once again, the old man looked surprised and then pleased, before thanking them and accepting the offer.

After eating and preparing for the day, he helped Nathan with his chores while Hannah packed a hearty lunch for the trip. As she did so, she wondered greatly at the words she thought she had heard that morning and at the pervading feeling she had that they were doing something very right.

As they finally knelt in the living room, Brother John began a prayer. Hannah marveled at the warmth in the room, wondering if the fire had somehow flared up. He was blessing their home, that it would be a safe haven for them and their children, that it would be guarded from evil while they were in it and that their service would be favored of the Lord all the days that they remembered him.

As he ended, the old man looked around. "Where are your children?" he asked.

"We don't have any," Nathan smiled, "but thank you just the same."

A twinkle suddenly appeared in his eyes. "Surely, one day you will have a quiver full," he declared. Then taking Hannah's young hands into his old and wrinkled ones, he spoke solemnly. "Never forget, my young lady, that in them you will be blessed. Always love them, as you wish your mother had loved you."

Hannah looked at the old man strangely. They had said nothing about her mother for him to know, yet once again the words warmed through her heart. Finally, the old gentleman excused himself from her presence and left with Nathan to town.

"Surely, it is a coincidence," Hannah thought to herself.

She watched from the window as they drove down the lane. It was very cold outside, though it still had not snowed. Considering the experience both curious and fascinating, she replayed the events of the morning over in her mind, wondering if it could possibly be true. Finally, smiling, Hannah drew her hands to her heart and whispered one of her favorite verses.

"As arrows are in the hand of a mighty man; so are children of the youth. *Happy is the man that hath his quiver full of them.*"

At her quiet words, Brother John turned around in the buggy and looked back over the distance of the lane to the house. He smiled, and then nodded and waved as they disappeared into the road and off around the corner to town. Hannah marveled at the odd circumstances once again, wondering at it greatly.

"Happy is the man," she whispered to herself.

Chapter Six

INGOTS!
JANUARY 1907

Nathan tied his horse to the post outside the bank and paused before going in. Something was nagging him, though he couldn't put his finger on what. All night he had tossed and turned, unable to sleep. From the moment he'd woken, he felt a restless and gnawing feeling that something wasn't right. Still, he couldn't think of what it might be. Pulling out his watch, he read five past the hour. He was late for his meeting. As he came into the bank, he saw Mark across the way.

"Nathan," Mark called out, "we've been waiting for you. Are you ready?"

Suddenly, another man approached from his side. "Excuse me, sir; might you be Nathan Layne?"

"Why, yes," he answered cautiously, not liking what he felt about this person. At the man's very presence, Nathan's feelings of uneasiness peaked, leaving him filled with a sense of dread. It really didn't make any sense. He had never met this fellow in his life.

"My name is Professor Caruthers, Daniel Caruthers of the Boston Museum, curator of Spanish artifacts. Certainly you've heard of me before," he said in tones of self-importance. "We've come across an item of special interest to our establishment and believe we have traced it to the Silver Falls area. I wonder if this might look familiar to you."

He produced a single ingot in his hand as Mark, curious of the situation, approached.

"Hey, look at that, Nathan; an ingot, just like the ones from the wreck."

The stranger whirled around to meet the statement, as Nathan fought back the panic he felt over Mark's words. Finally, taking the golden piece from the "professor's" hand, Nathan examined it closely, trying to think of a way to downplay the comment. It was very clear to him that this man, whoever he was, was not a "professor" or "curator" of any type and that his presence could well mean peril.

"It does look like those few you found, doesn't it?" he managed at last.

Mark was so pleased at the sight of it, as well as at the stranger's supposed position of renown. Picking up on his trusting nature, the man began to change his focus to Mark.

"You say you found some of these in a wreck. Are there more?"

"I suppose there might be. There weren't many left when we went there. I found barely enough to furnish my family with a home and buy an interest in the bank, meager though it was."

"Then your contribution to the bank wasn't very large from these ingots?"

"No, it wasn't enormous," Nathan broke in, handing the gold back, "but it was certainly sufficient. Now, if you'll excuse us, please; we are late for a meeting. Perhaps we can sit down with you another time and discuss the details. Right now, we have another commitment."

"Yes, of course," he conceded. Feeling obviously content with the information he had garnered, he fingered the gold contemptuously and gave Nathan a last knowing look. "Yes, perhaps we could meet very soon."

George was waiting for them, the secretary busily distributing the agendas, when they entered the meeting chamber. Though the business began quickly, Nathan's mind was swallowed up in the drama of the preceding moments. Who was that man, and how did he know about the ingots? How could he have connected them to the bank? And Mark's comment! He anguished over it. Both of their lives could be in danger because of it.

One thing seemed certain; he was looking for more of them. Maybe Nathan wasn't a perfect judge of character, but he had seen many people in the past consumed in murderous greed for gold, and something about this man was far too familiar of that experience.

Barely listening to what was said and not caring to contribute, he sat nervously through the next hour, examining the circumstances. How much could the man know? Were there more people involved than him? Did he know where they lived? And Hannah! She was home alone! At that realization, he began to worry about her until nothing else would register. The gold was dispensable; his wife was not.

With his mind in such turmoil, the meeting adjourned before he'd had a chance to fully figure out what he should do. Exiting the room, he felt mixed relief to see that the man was not waiting at the door, though his concern for his wife only heightened.

"Hey, I thought I'd surprise you."

Nathan nearly jumped at her touch. "Oh, Hannah, you can't imagine how glad I am to see you. Did you walk into town?"

"No, I came in with Davy. He needed to pick up a few things at Carroll's and I happened to be out in the lane as he was going by. It was a little spur of the moment. Is something the matter?"

Nathan had been visually surveying every corner of the bank, though the "professor" did not appear to be present, nor did he see him waiting outside.

"I hope not. Did you need anything in town?"

"No, I just thought I'd drop in and surprise you. It's such a pleasant day for January. I thought a drive home with you would be nice."

"Yes, I'm very glad you're here."

As they came out the doors, Nathan helped her into the carriage, all the while keeping his eyes open for anything out of the ordinary. Perhaps he was being a little overcautious, he chided himself.

As Hannah chatted on cheerily, Nathan remained in a cloud. It wasn't until they had passed their lane that her words finally began to register.

"Nathan, are you going to answer me?"

"I'm sorry, love; what was it you said?"

"I asked where we are going. I don't think you've listened to anything I've said at all, and you just passed our lane."

"Stay calm, Hannah, and speak quietly. We can't go home; we're being followed. Don't turn around! Just sit close to me and act as casually as you can."

Hannah scooted closer and snuggled into his arm. "How do you know we're being followed?" she whispered.

"I saw them on the last two turns. They're holding back, but they're definitely following us."

"Why would anyone want to do that?"

She would have taken the matter more lightly except for the nervousness in his voice and his tense manner. Even the horse, picking up on it through the reins, was restlessly tossing his head and prancing along the road, trying to break gait.

"Someone has found out about the gold and traced it to the bank, to Mark and myself. He claims to be a professor of some museum in Boston, seeking Spanish artifacts. I'm certain it's a front and a phony name. I don't know how he connected the gold to me or how much he knows about us. He approached me as I came into the bank this morning and showed me an ingot, questioning me about them. Before I could think of what to say, Mark identified the ingot as the ones from the wreck. I was concerned he might know where we lived and I worried about you being out there alone. I suppose the fact that he's following us confirms at least some of my fears."

"Where will we go then?"

"We can't go to anyone's house; it would put them in danger as well."

"It's six miles to Amberglen," she suggested.

"Yes, and perhaps by the time we get there we can think of a plan."

"We could have lunch and shop around. Maybe we could lose them."

"Not likely, Hannah; they're sure to be watching us closely."

"Well, what about the hotel? What if we checked into there and then snuck out at night?"

"And then what?"

"I don't know; we could go home, collect what gold is in the house, and get it out of Silver Falls altogether."

Nathan nodded slowly. "Our only option for that would be Uncle Adam."

"How much does he know?"

"Only that I have ingots I've been trading. He has no idea how many."

"Why do you suppose no one has ever traced them to his bank?"

Nathan smiled at his wife. "Because he melts them into bricks, Hannah. He has far more connections there than I will ever have here."

"But, surely, someone would get suspicious, wouldn't they?"

"No, the ingots should be completely safe with him until he has a chance to take care of them. Anyway, I don't know that the hotel idea will work, but so far it seems close to our only option, I suppose we can give it a try."

They rode the rest of the way in relative silence, only occasionally speaking of train schedules and how they could possibly transport the gold without raising suspicions. Upon arriving in town, the men casually followed them into a restaurant, ordering a small lunch themselves. After that, they watched them closely, sauntering into the hotel lobby as they checked in. Nathan continued to avoid eye contact or any other open acknowledgment of their presence. The more suspicious they were, the harder it would be to get away.

Requesting a room for two days in a volume which he hoped could be overheard by them both, Nathan paid for it all in advance. Afterwards, he went to see about getting the horse settled at the livery. He was hoping there would be some way out of it, but though the one man lagged behind in the lobby, the "professor" stuck to his trail. He found it difficult to stay even far enough ahead so as to be out of earshot.

After handing over his charge to the stable hand he paused and went back. "Young man," he called, once again loudly enough to be overheard. "I forgot to mention a problem with my horse."

Going back and picking up the bay's front hoof, Nathan pretended to examine it closely. "I'm from Silver Falls," he whispered, "and I'm being followed by two strangers; we're being watched even now. I'll pay you twenty dollars if you can have my horse harnessed and waiting at the north end of town by midnight tonight without anyone knowing a word about it."

"Twenty dollars!" the youth whispered back in an incredulous tone. "Yes, sir!"

"You'll have to take the back alley or they'll see you. I can only meet you there with the money if they have no idea I'm coming."

"Yes, sir," he offered more soberly, poking at the horse's hoof himself. His enthusiasm was encouraging and Nathan could only hope he would follow through.

Upon returning to their room he quietly explained the plan to Hannah as he crossed the floor to the window, peering from a corner of the curtain. "Now if we can just figure a way out of this room."

"Why? What could be the problem?"

"They heard our room number and they're watching us like hawks. That Caruthers fellow is across the street, watching the front and the other man is off to the side there, by that tree, watching our window. There is no back door."

Hannah walked to Nathan's position at the curtain and saw the man casually glance in their direction. "What about a room on the other side?" she asked.

Nathan nodded as he let the curtain slowly slip back into place. "Stay here, will you, love, and watch them while I see if we can get another room without their noticing. If either man leaves their place, then come downstairs and find me."

Quietly, he went back to the lobby and, finding it free of people, rented another room across the hall. Returning, he held his wife in his arms. "I guess we can only make ourselves comfortable, my love. It will likely be a long night."

The hours inched their way toward midnight, when Nathan finally gathered the sheets and carried them across the hall. Tying them into knots and securing them to the radiator below the window, he scanned the blackness outside. From his vantage point of the second floor, he could barely discern the silhouette of his horse and carriage already waiting at the edge of town.

"We've got to hurry and go quietly," he whispered. "I'll go down first. Quickly, love," he repeated, "and quietly."

Nathan silently slipped down their makeshift line, and then gave a tug for her. Gathering her skirts and ducking through the window, Hannah shuddered at the chill. The day had been unusually warm for this time of year and she hadn't planned on more than a quick trip into town and a drive home with her husband. She wasn't at all prepared for the frigid air that accosted her. Trying to wrap the sheet around her arm and leg as he had shown her, she took a last, long look in at the relative safety of the room before slowly lowering herself to the wintry ground below.

Picking their path through the blackness of the remaining three blocks, they made their way to the lad who was waiting in the faint light of a quarter moon just out from the clouds. Nathan thanked him, giving him the money and a warning.

"Remember, lad, not a word; and don't go home down Main Street. It won't be safe."

The boy nodded, gleefully running off the other direction, as Nathan urged the horse quietly around the back of town. Their hearts pounded as they crossed the opposite end of the main road and watched breathlessly for another two miles, though it appeared no one had seen them. The hush of the night was broken by their carriage alone. They were, for the moment at least, safely on their way home.

Chapter Seven

AND THEN THERE WAS ONE . . .
FEBRUARY 1907

"Nathan! Hannah!"

The train had barely stopped, but Adam Layne had spotted them through a window from his place on the platform and was uncharacteristically animated, calling out their names, trying to get their attention. It worked, and as soon as they could exit the rail car Nathan's uncle embraced them warmly.

"Thank goodness you are here," he stated.

"We weren't expecting anyone to meet us," Nathan began, "but it is a pleasant surprise."

Uncle Adam looked grave and, leading Hannah to the car, he saw her comfortably seated and the door securely closed. When he was certain she was out of earshot, he turned to his nephew and broke the bitter news.

"Pleasantries aside, it is your safety that concerns us most now. Andrew wired me the day after you left," he was quiet, appearing lost in his thoughts. "Mark has been shot, and the whole countryside out there is reeling from the shock of it."

"What?" Nathan exclaimed in disbelief. "Is he alive? What happened?"

"He's alive, but not well. I don't know how you want to break this to Hannah, but Andrew said they'd be sending a letter shortly with more news. In the meantime, we're to keep you here under all circumstances. Your life may be in grave danger there, Nathan; you mustn't go back."

"Oh, I'm certain it is," he agreed, "but I thought Mark would be safe." Nathan shook his head, obviously disturbed from the news. "It's all my fault, I'm afraid. Had I stayed to confront the situation, this probably would never have happened."

"You sound like you know more than you're saying."

Nathan shrugged his shoulders in bewilderment. "I thought they were only after me; I had no idea they would go after Mark."

"The gold?" Adam asked.

"Yes, or at least I assume so. A man came into the bank with an ingot a few days ago, looking for more. When I left after our meeting, they followed me."

"They?"

"Yes, the one man said he was a curator from a museum in Boston; he was alone in the bank, but there was another man with him outside afterwards."

Adam scowled at the news. "It doesn't sound like they were up to any good."

"No, and I'm sure the museum story was merely a cover. Oh, but I should have stayed."

"Why? So they could shoot you too? You know these types, Nathan; they will stop at nothing in their greed."

"Yes, I suppose," he whispered, instinctively looking around the area and then running his hands nervously over his face. Nathan was understandably shaken. "I wish I knew more about Mark," he said at last.

"Well, a letter shouldn't be too long in the waiting."

Their bags were retrieved and with great effort loaded into the back of the car, as the news was at last broken to Hannah. All the way to the bank, Adam tried to fill them in on what very few details he knew. It was after hours when they arrived, the building dark and vacant, as their uncle secured the gold into the safety of the vault.

"Is this the last of it?" Adam asked.

Nathan grimaced. "It's the last of what was in the house."

Despite the drama of the last few days, Adam smiled and shook his head. "I don't think I even want to know."

Once home, they read the telegram over and over again, trying to find within its contents any shred of information that might enlighten them more as, all the while, Nathan fought the sting of his mounting self-condemnation.

"This is my fault, Hannah. I shouldn't have left."

"No, it isn't, Nathan; you can't be blamed for the actions of that evil man. Staying home to be killed yourself wouldn't have done a thing to guarantee protection for Mark or anyone else." Hannah looked over the telegram again. "Poor Mark," she whispered at last. "It will be torture waiting to find out if he's all right."

It was nearly a week before a letter finally arrived. Taking the same course as the trains they had come on, the information was five days old, though never had they received a post with more anticipation.

February 9, 1907

Dear Nathan and Hannah,

We trust you are there safely and I'm sure you've heard from Adam that Mark was shot and seriously wounded. He seems to be healing well enough now. Peter has little doubt that he'll recover, as the rounds went clear through, apparently missing his vitals and landing in the wall behind him. For now, all three wounds appear to be clear.

Odd as it may sound, a stranger broke into his house the night after you left, demanding gold, of all things! It was a tremendous scare! Mark tried to tell him he didn't have any, but the man was crazed with fury at his answer and began shooting. Fortunately, Carolyn was spared any injury, and the children were safely in another part of the house.

Eventually, the stranger fled into the night, and the next morning Peter found your place had been completely torn apart. Someone had broken the windows near the door in the kitchen and made a complete mess of the place. Shelves were emptied onto the floor, furniture overturned and pretty much everything was as upside down as it could get. Many things were broken, and we trust there wasn't anything there that can't be replaced. The animals are fine, they were at our place, but it will probably be days before we can get it entirely put back together. Your father has fixed the broken windows but that will be all that happens for a while. Quite frankly, right now most people are staying indoors and out of the way and our family is no exception.

Please stay where you're at until further notice. We'll write as we can to let you know what we've found, and will send a wire as soon as we feel your return would be safe. The sheriffs from Silver Falls and the surrounding towns are doing their best to resolve this and restore order and quiet once again to the area. Please stay put and don't worry about things here; we'll take care of it all as best we can.

With love, Mother

"Thank heavens he is going to be okay!" Hannah exclaimed.

Nathan agreed, though he still couldn't shake the belief that, had he stayed, Mark would not have been harmed at all. There was little to do now but lay low and try to remain calm.

Uncle Adam made short work disposing of the ingots and depositing their value into Nathan's account; however, the cash would need to stay put for now. There was no sense raising questions over large transfers at the moment, or giving any more possible incentive for the strangers to pry further into the matters of the bank. All things considered, Nathan applied his efforts at appearing calmer than he actually felt while keeping things as low key and peaceful as possible.

❧

Two more weeks of waiting crept by, and then one day, after spending time in town, they returned to Adam Layne's house in the chill of a mid-winter's evening.

"Uncle Adam, Aunt Nanette," Hannah called, "we're home." The house remained quiet to her call. "I wonder where they went."

"I don't know, but it mustn't have been all that long ago. There are still coals in the fireplace."

Walking into the kitchen, Nathan noticed the stack of mail on the table with a letter addressed to him on top of the pile. More news had arrived from home, this time from his father. Anxiously, he opened the envelope and read it aloud.

February 25, 1907

Dear Nathan,

How are you, son? Mark is doing well. He is back home now and hopes to return to work before too long. With the both of you gone, George is feeling overwhelmed by the responsibility of the bank, wondering if he was to be the next target of aggression, though no one has seen anything more of the stranger with the gun.

Sheriff Mackay discovered the body of a man down at the point a few days ago and brought him to Peter before sending him to the coroner in Amber Glen. He had apparently been there a while, as well as the leftover fragments of a small skiff strewn over the rocks. Why anyone would be so foolish as to trust their persons around that treacherous cove in the depths of winter is beyond me. Peter said that the man appeared to have drowned, though he was also frozen through. The coroner will know more and said he would be sure to keep Peter informed.

Not being able to identify him, they came to Mark and asked if he could establish the stranger as the gunman who had broken into his home. We were all in high hopes that it was, so that the town might settle down and people could get back to normal living, but Mark said he couldn't be sure. It had been so dark that night and he hadn't seen any details of the man's features. However, he said he did resemble a professor of some sort who had come into the bank asking about golden ingots. The stranger on the beach had several of the same gold pieces on him, so the sheriff feels certain that the two are somehow connected.

Either way, the trouble seems to have passed for now, with no further incidents that we know of. It is probably safe here; though

I think it would be best if you stayed put a little longer to be sure. We'll wire you if anything further comes up.

The weather has been very cold, one arctic storm after another and not at all conducive to strangers wandering the countryside. Your mother has worked hard over the last few days and has your house pretty well put back together. While a few things are broken, it doesn't appear that anything is missing. Under the circumstances, we should probably count our blessings that it wasn't any worse. We hope to see you before too much longer, as soon as it is safe.

Take care of yourselves.

Love, Dad

Nathan slowly folded the letter and put it back into the envelope as a gentle feeling of peace began to settle over him. He still had plenty of questions to answer in his own mind, but overall he felt relieved from this particular piece of news.

"I think we'll be okay now, Hannah."

Hannah shook her head and stared out the window. "It could have been you, Nathan; they could have killed you. I don't feel so sure about it at all. Oh, I'm glad the gold is gone from our house! How is it that such a thing can inspire people to such violence? I can't understand it at all. Mark has a wife and children who depend on him. Don't they stop to think about that? Doesn't it matter to them at all? What is wrong with these people? Oh, I don't think I can go back."

Tossing a few logs onto the remaining embers, Nathan considered the situation during the several minutes it took him to build the fire back up in the hearth. Eventually, once the chill that had held the room so ransom began to give way to a warm comfort, he rose and took a seat on the couch.

"Come sit by the fire with me, won't you, Hannah?" he offered, clearing a place for her as well. Once settled, he pulled her closer. "I really think it'll be all right; I feel peaceful about it."

"It is just so unfair! Who do those people think they are to be shooting others and tearing houses apart and threatening innocent people?"

"Yes, and all for the love of gold, Hannah; but we're safe now and we need to move on."

"Nathan, they could have killed us both."

He looked off into the fire, considering the truth of her words and wondering what he could say that might calm her nerves and change her focus. "It is the truest test, isn't it? It's easy to be kind to those who love us, but to those who hate us or abuse us and are filled with evil, to let it go when they wrong us, that is a challenge," he mused thoughtfully.

"It still isn't fair."

"No, it isn't; I agree. I suppose that's what makes it such a test," he smiled.

Hannah looked up at him, a little in awe of the person she had married and amazed that he could even speak of something like letting this go. Finally she turned again to the fire, watching the flames dance around and through the logs. After a long while, she spoke again.

"I still don't want to go back, but more than that, I wish your parents had raised me, Nathan. I wish that I could have learned the lessons for myself that your father has taught you."

A large grin swept over his face as he pulled her closer and kissed her forehead. "Well, I'm certainly glad they didn't," he laughed. "I would have had a dickens of a time getting a marriage license for my sister."

Hannah managed a smile too as he brushed the curls from her face, giving her a gentle squeeze. The fire was pleasant and the house so quiet. They were there without further obligation and it might be days before there would be any real need to leave.

"Let her have some time," Nathan thought to himself. "Let us both have some time."

Looking across the room and into the fire, he considered again the words of the letter. Apparently, "Professor Caruthers," or whatever his actual name might have been, would not be harassing them further. That might have been more of a comfort, except for the unfortunate fact that there were two men who had followed them to Amber Glen, not just one. Who was the other man, and how much did he know?

Nathan mused a little further while his curiosity of the situation only grew. Finally, he gave his wife another gentle squeeze.

"We can stay a while longer, Hannah love, if it will make you feel more at ease. Surely, we will be home soon enough."

Chapter Eight

A New Dawn
March 1907

The Laynes arrived back in Silver Falls in early March and began the task of trying to assess the damage and put the few leftovers back into their rightful places. It was, even then, a little nerve wracking for Hannah, wondering if anyone might come back and feeling so violated at the trespass of their home.

It had nearly blown over in town, and even Mark's family was returning to normal. Thus, it came as a surprise to be sleeping peacefully one night when her husband suddenly bolted up, scrambled out of bed, and dressed as quickly as he could.

Startled from her sleep, she began calling after him. "Nathan, what's the matter? What are you doing?"

"I've got to leave!"

Thinking he must surely be doing this in his sleep, she tried to calm him. "Honey, come back to bed; it is only the middle of the night."

"No, Hannah; Dad is gone. I need to go help my mother."

Shocked out of the remainder of her sleepiness, she too began to get up and prepare to leave. Hannah called after him to wait, but he was already out the door, leaving her in blackness as the clock in the front room chimed at two a.m. Realizing that she was on her own, she slowed down and began trying to think things through. Nathan was naturally intuitive, but this seemed a little too unreal. Surely, it was just the effects of a dream.

"Well," she sighed, "if something really has happened, then what will we need?"

She realized, as an approaching wave of nausea began to sweep over her, that if she was going to be of use to anyone, she would have to take care of her own needs first. She had been wondering at the symptoms for several days and though she was fairly sure of their source, she felt that now was not the time to break such news. She would need to save it and keep it to herself a little longer. She longed to share her suspicions with Nathan, but it appeared there may be tragedy to deal with at the moment.

Wondering at the unusually long string of drama they'd experienced lately, Hannah hurried with the rest of her things, left the house and, by the light of the moon, picked her way through the fields to Nathan's parents'. The air was cold and frosty and the ground still frozen with winter. In the distance, she could see the house all aglow against the darkness and realized with dread that, somehow, Nathan must have been right.

Andrew Layne had been a pillar of integrity in the Silver Falls Community from its earliest days. Consequently, a great number of people turned out to his funeral to offer their last respects and try to comfort his grieving family.

Everyone was numb with shock over the loss, but no one like Sarah, as she groped from one moment to the next. Andrew was her husband, the man she had known and held and loved for nearly forty years, her confidant and companion, her comfort and support. While the minister had reminded them all that it was only temporary, that Andrew's good soul had merely gone on ahead of them to a happier place, it was little comfort to her. The man that she loved felt completely gone from all that she had experience to feel and know.

Time, of course, would eventually dull the pain, but it would first have to dull the memory. For now, that memory and comfort were all far too sharp and painfully missed. The loneliness she would face would surely be the greatest trial of her life.

All of the Laynes worked through their various stages of loss in different ways and at different times, Nathan taking it especially hard. He and Andrew had been so close, and Hannah mourned almost as much for his loss as she did for her own. It was a time of great sorrow.

One night early in April, not long after the funeral, they were sitting before the fire in quiet thought, when Hannah felt another wave of nausea compelling her to go in search of the biscuits in the pantry. It always seemed to come worse at night, and she found the best relief to be a simple biscuit and sleep. As she retook her seat, slowly nibbling at the bit of bread, Nathan noticed for the first time that she was looking pale.

"Hannah, love, are you feeling well?"

"I'll be all right by morning, I'm sure. If you don't mind, I think I'll turn in early though; I'm really tired."

Nathan began thinking. She had been tired a lot lately, taking naps during the day, waking up late in the morning and going to bed early. It wasn't like her and he wondered if she was worn out from trying to help the family, or perhaps if she was coming down with something serious. She generally stayed in her nightclothes as well, much longer in the mornings and sooner at night than usual. He wondered how he hadn't picked up on it before now.

There wasn't time to ask more, for she had already left the room and climbed into bed, trying to gain a quick respite from her sickness. Though it was only a little before eight, he decided to follow.

"Are you sure you're all right?"

"I'll be fine, Nathan; I'm just very tired. Things have been too busy lately."

Settling close to her, he felt her cheek and forehead, though she was cool.

"Hannah, you don't look well. Please, don't feel you have to keep anything from me."

"It's all right; you've had enough to think about."

"Hannah, you are keeping something from me."

"I suppose I have. I've been so tired; I didn't want to burden you with it."

Bracing himself for the worst, he ventured the question. "What is it?"

This felt so unromantic to her. It wasn't the way she had planned to tell him at all. She had hoped to have a cozy evening when she was feeling a little better, and after he wasn't so burdened with his own cares. But here she was, in the throes of exhaustion and feeling desperately nauseated. All she wanted to do was try to escape into the relief of sleep, and Nathan was breathing in her face.

"Please, can we talk about this in the morning?" she asked in a half moan, as she rolled over away from him, trying to get some fresh air.

Nathan only worried more. If something happened to her . . . he felt he couldn't bear even the thought.

"Should I get Peter? Hannah, if something happened to you, I couldn't endure it, especially not right now."

The worry in his voice made her turn back. Putting her arm around him, despite her misery, and pulling him close, she whispered.

"Nathan, it's all right. I think I'm expecting a baby is all. I really want to talk to you about it, but right now I am feeling so ill and exhausted that *I* can hardly bear it. Please, let me go to sleep."

At first he was sure he hadn't heard her right, but as he listened to the sentence over and over in his mind, he realized that it was exactly what she had said. Tenderly kissing her on the forehead, he settled himself in bed to spend a long and happily sleepless night staring at the ceiling, wondering about the rest.

It was, perhaps, one of the greatest sacrifices he ever made for her that night, fighting back a tidal wave of questions in order to let her rest. As he lay there quietly in the darkness, consumed with wondering, he felt the first shreds of sublime happiness he'd had in months. It all made so much sense now. He wondered how he hadn't picked up on it before.

Chapter Nine

HELP FOR HANNAH
MAY 1907

By late spring, Nathan could feel the movements with his hand, and by June Hannah was beginning to wonder if the baby would ever stop rolling and kicking. She was getting uncomfortable and wondered at the prospects of twins, knowing they'd happened before in both families. Oblivious to her discomfort, Nathan loved watching her, excited at the thought of being a parent and admiring how feminine she seemed, more so than before.

By the time she had reached her fifth month, the movements were constant and Hannah began to wonder how much larger she could get. The ladies at church, ever full of advice and information, solicited or not, assured her that people merely carry their babies differently and that she must be the type that carries hers "out front." However, this was only said after someone else had asked her how far overdue she was.

To make matters worse, she felt constantly and voraciously hungry and was having trouble getting even the simplest of her chores completed without ending up drained and out of breath. Finally, in July, with the harvest season around the corner and feeling completely overwhelmed, she brought the subject up to Nathan.

"I can't even keep up with my appetite, let alone my chores," she told him.

"You have been eating a lot, love."

"But Peter said it must be twins. He said that I've barely gained enough weight for one baby and told me to eat more. He hardly has to encourage it, Nathan; I feel starved almost constantly, and I'm getting so huge. I look like an elephant."

"You look very much a woman, Hannah. It makes my heart thrill to look at you. I'm sorry you don't feel as beautiful as you look."

Hannah had to laugh. "Beautiful" was about the furthest thing from what she felt.

"Maybe we can find some help," he offered, "or hire someone to bring in the crops."

They talked over the possibilities, and the next morning Nathan spoke to his mother. Sarah was overjoyed to have something to throw her energies into. She spread the word among the other relatives as well, and they began cooking a little extra to their meals and bringing a portion over every now and then.

By the end of July, Peter, upon examining her, just shook his head. The calipers no longer stretched far enough to measure the span, and the babies (there was no question now that there were two) were in such constant motion that he could never be sure where one's foot left off and the other's head began. He and Nathan were both trying to help her off the examining table, when a knock came at the office door.

Peter excused himself to answer it, while Hannah tried to keep the tears from escaping. She was overjoyed at the prospect of having two babies at once, but the physical challenges were becoming great. Combined with the heat of the summer, she was beginning to feel faint and unstable, which only made her frightened for herself and the babies too.

A few moments later, Peter emerged back into the room followed by a young woman.

"Nathan, this is Alannah. I'm sorry; I don't remember your last name."

"Jensen," she replied.

"Yes, that's right. She's looking for work; do you know if there are any openings at the bank?"

Nathan nodded a hello. "Not that I know of, but Mark would have a better idea on that." Turning to the girl, he asked. "What kind of work are you looking for?"

"Anything that is an honest living would be fine."

Something in her answer caught even Hannah's attention for the element of sincerity.

"Where are you living that we could get back with you?"

She looked down at her shoes, then back up and out the window. "I suppose I could stay around the general store for the day, if you think you would know by then."

"We're all closing down for lunch right now," Nathan announced. "Why don't you join us and we could discuss it further. Actually," he added, "if you're not opposed to domestic work, we might be able to use your help at home. Join us for lunch and we'll figure it all out."

Sarah Layne had lunch ready for them by the time they all arrived, but Hannah, too exhausted to stay up any longer, sought the refuge of her bed. Once everyone else was settled around the table, with the introductions and small talk over, the four remaining adults began to discuss the possibilities.

Peter decided that he could use someone in the office one or two days a week to help with the bookwork and other little odd jobs. Mrs. Layne, not wanting to give up her involvement with Hannah and the babies, offered Alannah room and board in exchange for housekeeping. Nathan also felt that there might always be "a thing or two" that he or Hannah could use help with in the garden or yard or around the house. All in all, everyone felt fairly pleased at the prospects, and Alannah, in her very quiet way, could not say thank you enough.

At last, she and Sarah Layne left to see the house and settle her in, leaving Nathan at the table and Peter standing near the window in the kitchen, watching them disappear in the distance.

"She seems like a nice girl," Nathan remarked. "I'm glad we were able to help her."

"Isn't she beautiful?" Peter asked, still watching her from the window as she crossed the brook to his home.

Nathan looked at his brother in surprise. "I hadn't noticed."

"Well I did! I was almost afraid to offer her the work for fear I'd stare at her the whole time, and then when Mother offered her room and board," Peter laughed and shook his head. "I thought I was going to have an anxiety attack on the spot. It will be nice though, having someone else around to bring a little cheer back into the house.

Mother has been thriving on helping Hannah. I really think it has given her a new purpose in life for now. She much prefers being here than at home."

Nathan nodded his agreement before changing the subject. "Peter, what about Hannah? She seems so frail and unstable. Do you think she's going to be all right?"

"I think she's probably feeling more miserable than she's letting on to," Peter agreed; "but the babies appear to be strong and healthy, and they're in good position, so far as I can tell. I still say she is off on her dates though. She can't possibly be due in October."

Hannah wondered herself how she would ever make it to October. It was only July yet and a full eleven and a half weeks until the babies were due, according to her dates. She couldn't sleep well, it being impossible to be on her stomach as well as on her back. When she so much as rested more than a minute on her back, she had feelings of suffocating and losing consciousness. The only position left was on her side, or maybe "sides" was a better description, for she could only remain on each about fifteen minutes before her arm and leg would begin to fall asleep. Heaving over her cumbersome mass, she would then begin the process on the other side, continuing this constantly day and night. She was also always hungry, but could eat only mere tidbits at a time for the lack of space left in her stomach. It, along with the rest of her insides, was being crowded beyond belief. She continued on this way for several more weeks, getting all the more crowded and uncomfortable with each passing day.

On a mid-August night, early in the morning hours, she once again heaved herself over in bed to let the circulation revive. Nathan had grown accustomed to the tossing and turning and was in his own utter exhaustion from the work of the harvest. When she had rolled this last time, however, her stomach pressed up against his back and the babies began kicking him as well.

"Please, stop kicking me," he requested sleepily.

"I'm not kicking you."

"Your stomach is kicking me," he mumbled in his exhaustion.

"Your babies are kicking you, Nathan, and they are kicking me as well, constantly! I will be so glad when this is over. I don't see how

I can endure it much longer. I feel ready to burst and I keep dreaming that I am giving birth to litters of puppies and kittens."

"I'm sorry, Hannah," he offered groggily, gathering up his pillow and a blanket and taking it to the front room to sleep on the rug. At least there he could rest undisturbed.

Hannah felt a little bruised over it at first, but realized he would never make it through the next day if he wasn't able to get some rest from his toil in the heat of the fields. Besides, she consoled herself, there was more room this way.

As the days wore on, Peter began coming morning and night to check on her, declaring each time that it couldn't be much longer. She clung to his words as though they were her only hope and waited out each day with all the patience she could muster, repeating over and over, "this too shall pass."

Chapter Ten

BLESSINGS OF OMISSION
AUGUST 1907

Alannah sat quietly, amazed that anyone could be sleeping so late in the day, and even more astonished by how enormous and disproportionate Hannah appeared. Sarah Layne had some of her own work to catch up on and, since Peter's orders were that Hannah could not be left alone, Alannah was the one commissioned to keep watch on this particular day.

She glanced over at the nursery, all trimmed and ready to receive its charges. Two bassinets were decorated with ruffles and ribbons and two diaper-stackers were filled to the point of bulging with new diapers and freshly knitted woolen soakers. A changing table and dresser stood in stately newness, and little embroidered outfits, hung out on their individual racks, were on full display. It was all beautiful and so welcoming, though Alannah felt instead a very deep ache creep over her heart.

"Good morning," Hannah ventured sleepily, "are you to be my guard for the day?"

"Mrs. Layne had some other things to do. I hope that's all right."

"Yes, it's fine; in fact, it's wonderful. I've been wanting to get to know you better. Had I been up to my old self, we would probably be chums by now."

"Can I get you anything, Mrs. Layne?"

"Yes, a little breakfast would be nice, only Mrs. Layne is Nathan's mother," she smiled. "I'm Hannah."

Alannah acknowledged the request and returned after a few minutes. "Can I do anything for you, Hannah? You look so . . . uncomfortable."

Hannah laughed. "I'm desperately uncomfortable, but listening to someone talk at least keeps me occupied and helps me not to dwell on it. Why don't you tell me about yourself? How did you come to be in Silver Falls?"

Being very quiet and shy, Alannah replied simply. "I was looking for work."

"That's right, I remember that part, but where were you before? Where were you raised?"

"Before coming here, I was living with my mother and her friends. I recently came of age and decided to go out on my own."

"You're twenty-one then?"

"Yes. Your nursery is lovely."

Hannah noticed a sadness in her comment. "Nathan's mother has been so good to humor me on it. She regularly changes it all around and adds more diapers to it as though her efforts might somehow speed up this whole process."

Alannah smiled and relaxed a little. "Where is your mother, Hannah?"

"She died when I was a baby."

"What about your father?"

"He died with my mother; there was an accident. What about you?"

She was quiet again. "Last I knew, my mother was in Albany, and I don't know about my father. He left before I was born."

"What about brothers or sisters?"

"Lilly," Alannah acknowledged quietly.

"Where is she now?"

"She died when she was twelve."

"Oh, I'm sorry," Hannah offered. "Do you have any other brothers or sisters?"

"Not living."

"Oh." She was beginning to sense that "family" might not be the happiest topic for Alannah and so decided to take a little different approach. "How is it working out for you, staying with Mother and Peter?"

"They've been very kind," she began. "It's more than I could have hoped for. It might give me a new perspective on life yet."

"What about Peter?" she ventured, having heard of his interest in her and hoping she would volunteer more information than the minimum.

"He seems very nice, and he is pleasant to work for. The job he offered me has been interesting and has helped out tremendously. He is so patient with my mistakes," she smiled, as though at some secret thought.

"What are your goals, Alannah; your plans for the future?"

"I would like to be independent and not have to rely on anyone."

"What about marriage?"

"I don't think I could ever marry," she stated in a tone of finality. "I don't think I would be the type." Just then Hannah grimaced. "Are you all right?"

"Oh, it's only another pain, one more. Now there are back aches too." As the pain built in intensity, Hannah gripped the edge of the bed. "Could you rub my lower back Alannah, please? It's really hurting."

Alannah did so, but after another half minute the pain began to subside and Hannah announced that it felt better. They chatted a few minutes more when her back began to hurt again, and once again Alannah rubbed it. After the fifth or sixth time Alannah excused herself and soon Nathan came in from the fields to sit with her.

"Hi, love. Alannah said she needed to run home. How are you feeling?"

"Oh, alright, I guess. Could you rub my back please, Nathan?"

"Sure. It's nice to have a little break."

"A little break," she muttered. "Do you suppose I chased her off?"

"She did seem rather in a hurry to leave. What were you talking about?"

"I don't remember; her plans for the future, I think. Rub harder honey, please!" she asked urgently.

"Are you all right?"

She didn't answer, but rather was holding her breath against the pain. At last, she blew out a long sigh as it subsided.

"Oh, Nathan," she cried out, "I don't know that I can endure backaches on top of everything else. I've tried to be cheerful, honest I have, but there are still more than six weeks to go. If I have to endure this for that long, I don't know that I can do it. Just when I get used to one pain, another type comes and I wonder how many more there can possibly be."

"When I'm in pain, I try to count my blessings."

She gave him a completely futile look. "Blessings?" she repeated blankly. "Well, I'm thankful that you built a strong house and that the roof isn't falling in."

"That sounds a little strange. Why would you be particularly thankful for that?"

"Because, if the roof fell in, I would never be able to move fast enough to get out of the way. So I'm thankful for the strong roof."

"Okay."

"And I'm thankful you built the house under the trees. If it had been built in the sun, I would be even hotter than I am now. I'm thankful that no one in our family is ill, and I'm thankful that we don't have tornadoes in Silver Falls."

He looked at her doubtfully and then smiled. "Are there any other things you feel particularly grateful for?"

Hannah grimaced in pain and took a deep breath. "I'm thankful that you're very strong and can apply that strength to my back. Please, Nathan, rub it again, hard. Harder, Nathan!"

He rubbed as hard as he could and couldn't imagine how it might possibly feel good, though it appeared to make the pain go away. As she breathed out another long breath, he could almost feel a relief of sorts himself.

"I'm thankful," she began out of breath, "that I don't have the chicken pox right now, and I'm thankful there are only six and a half more weeks instead of seven, and I'm thankful that the house isn't on fire, and I'm thankful that I don't have warts on the end of my nose, and I'm thankful that I don't have the flu right now, that could be considerably more miserable. Though, maybe I shouldn't speak too soon, as I am feeling a little more nauseated than usual. But I'm thankful I'm not covered in boils like Job, and that my legs aren't broken and my hair hasn't all fallen out, yet. Would you still love me if I were bald, Nathan?" she asked, as though she earnestly meant every word of it, to which Nathan out and out laughed.

"Come now, Hannah. These are mostly blessings of omission."

"Oh, but I am truly grateful for them. And I'm grateful that my teeth haven't fallen out or broken from my grinding them in the night, and I'm thankful that my headaches aren't worse than they are, and I'm thankful I can still breathe ever so slightly, though I dream all the time that I'm suffocating in my sleep. Nathan, do you suppose I'm really pregnant?"

"What?"

"I was just wondering whether I might have lost my mind and only imagined that I was pregnant when actually I've gotten extremely fat and this is all a permanent condition. Please rub my back again, hard. Another thing," she gasped, "that . . . I'm . . . thankful . . . for . . . is . . . that . . . my . . . back . . ." she held her breath another moment, grimacing against the pain, before blowing it out again and lying limp on the bed, "is that my back isn't broken," she finished quietly.

"Come now, Hannah. What about life and your health? Surely, you can be grateful for something that is a bona fide blessing."

"I'm not feeling healthy, and just now death feels like more of a blessing than life."

"Oh, love; it can't be as bad as that, can it?"

"Nathan!" she began impatiently, "do you know what it is like to go for weeks on end without ever being able to get a full breath, always feeling as though you were about to suffocate? Breathing is a pretty basic desire to my thinking. Or what about being utterly famished, only to feel full after eating mere spoonfuls, and then to feel famished again in another twenty minutes? Or to have all of your lower joints and muscles constantly hurting and aching, or to not get a decent hour of sleep for months at a time? Breathing, eating, and sleeping seem like fairly basic necessities. Even my skin hurts, and the babies are kicking me constantly in all directions at once. Do you know what it's like to be kicked in the lungs or the liver or the bladder, or to have your heart start pounding frantically for no reason, and to feel so constantly faint and fatigued and exhausted and sore and emotional and frustrated and worried and itchy and unstable and hot and nauseated? And on top of all that, to have your hands and arms and feet constantly falling asleep and going completely numb? I will be honest with you, my dear husband; I don't think you can even imagine it. Oh, why did Eve have to eat that fruit?"

Nathan chuckled to himself. "I'm sorry, Hannah, but it can't go on much longer. Try to remember that scripture you loved so well. 'Children are an heritage of the Lord, and happy is the man that hath his quiver full of them.' Remember?"

"Nathan," she began, grimacing against the pain once more. "I would like to see that man's 'quiver.' I'm sure . . . he never . . . had . . . such . . . a . . . quiver as full as this . . ." she blew out another breath. "And I would like to see him just try to be happy in it, and then write another scripture about it!"

"All right," he conceded. "Let's talk about after the babies are born. What is the first thing you want to do after the babies are born?"

"Oh, that's easy, lie on my stomach. And after that I want to take one hundred of the most enormously, deep breaths you've ever seen, and then I want to go outside and run around the barn five times and jump up and down and ride Dolly and go swimming in the ocean, through the waves, and could you rub my back again?"

"Hannah, maybe I should go get Peter."

"No! Please don't leave me. I feel so unstable . . . There, that's better. And then I'm going to eat an enormous, gigantic meal, and sleep! I'm going to sleep, on my stomach, for three days straight and get up and get dressed every morning thereafter, and do for myself instead of being done for and imposing on everyone else and . . ."

She would have gone on longer, but there was a knock at the door and her listening ear had left to answer it. She could hear Peter's voice and then Alannah's and then Nathan's all in quiet tones until, at last, Peter came into the room, followed by the others.

"Well, well, Dr. Layne," Hannah began, trying to sound at least a pinch cheerful. "How are we doing today?"

"I'm fine, Hannah, and how are you?"

Looking at Nathan and then back to Peter, she managed a contemptuous smile.

"Why, fine, Peter. Never felt better in my life. Whatever could lead you to ask such a silly question?"

He looked bewildered before realizing the sarcasm behind her answer. "Are we feeling as badly as that?" he smiled.

Hannah tried to smile back, but at the moment her back was starting to hurt again and instead she knit her brows and replied through clenched teeth, "I . . . don't . . . know . . . about . . . we, Peter . . . but . . . oh, please . . . help me!"

By that point, Peter had his hand on her stomach and was checking his watch, while Nathan rubbed her back.

"For heaven's sake, Hannah, breathe, breathe! Don't hold your breath!"

As the pain subsided, she felt she couldn't stand it any longer and cried out. "Oh, Peter! I can't possibly endure this for six more weeks. Please, help me!"

"Six weeks? Not likely; you're in labor, Hannah, and from the looks of it, it shouldn't be too much longer, maybe a few more hours."

"Labor?" they chimed together.

"I thought labor was supposed to happen here in the front," Hannah stated, "not in my back."

Peter chuckled. "It is happening up there, but your muscles are so stretched that the majority of the pain is registering in your back. Feel here the next time your back begins to hurt and you'll feel the muscles tighten."

He had almost finished examining her when the pain began again. Peter checked his watch. Two and a half minutes had passed. "Breathe, Hannah! Don't hold your breath!"

"Like this," Alannah broke in, kneeling next to her and showing her exactly how to get through the pain.

Peter glanced at her in surprise. "That's right, Hannah, follow Alannah; she's doing it just right. Nathan, you'd better run and get Mother; we may need her help once the babies start coming."

Nathan had been in a sort of daze from the time Peter had pronounced the word "labor," and it was only when the doctor urgently asked him to "hurry and get Mother!" that he came to his senses at all.

Alannah was indispensable, as well as Sarah, once she arrived, and only Nathan was left to wonder at it all. Finally, hearing Hannah's cries and groans, he could stand it no longer and went back into the bedroom to find something, anything he could do to help. It ended up being little more than holding her hand and whispering words of encouragement. After what seemed like forever, Peter held a small infant upside down and began clearing its mouth and nose. Soon, the baby began to scream.

"Congratulations, Nathan, Hannah; it's a girl." Peter was quickly taking care of the necessities, wiping the baby, checking her thoroughly, and cutting the cord. Finally, he handed her to Sarah, who wrapped the screaming infant up and handed her to Nathan.

"Oh, Hannah, she's beautiful! Look at her." He held her close for his wife to see, but Hannah's own happy tears clouded her vision and her words wouldn't quite come out. Instead, she gazed in a complete wonder at their new little daughter.

Soon, the pains returned and the whole process repeated itself, eventually presenting the second baby.

"It's another girl," Peter called out. "Hello, little one," he said cheerfully. "I believe I've seen you before." Repeating the same process as for the first, he eventually handed her to Alannah. "You'd better mark those two, Nathan or you'll never keep track of who is who."

Sarah took the baby and held her close for Hannah to see. "Well now, Hannah, do you want to hold your little daughter?" she asked, placing the baby on her tummy.

With all of the commotion going on in the room over the new, little girls, no one noticed the look of concern on Peter's face until, at last, Alannah happened to glance over.

"Why, Peter, what's the matter?"

"Something is wrong here," he mumbled. "I don't know what it . . ."

Frozen, they all stared at him, waiting for Peter to finish what he was going to say. Then, suddenly, Hannah began to groan in pain.

"Mother, take the baby!" she pleaded, grimacing once more.

Examining her, Peter shook his head. "I think there's another baby in there . . ." Checking it out further, he announced. "Yes, there is, though it feels breech. Alannah, do you remember what I taught you about turning a baby?"

"Yes, I think so."

"Then help me after this contraction, and at the next one, be ready to push."

They tried the procedure, going through the process over and over for nearly an hour before having any success. Finally, in the end, a very limp and blue baby emerged. Peter worked on him for what seemed an eternity before he finally took a breath and let out a short, weak whimper. He was very small.

After the doctor's all too brief examination, Nathan walked over and took the baby from his brother, bundling him and bringing him at last to Hannah.

"Look, Hannah, we have a little son, too. Three children, love, and they are so beautiful; I can hardly believe it."

The room was quiet as Peter solemnly finished up his work.

"You are so somber, Peter. Is everything all right?" Alannah asked.

"The girls should be fine," Peter began. "They are robust and strong. You had to be off on your dates though, Hannah. It's not possible that they could be this large and still have nearly seven weeks to go. They are surprisingly robust and healthy."

"What about our boy?" Hannah asked.

Peter took a deep breath and blew it out slowly, before giving a sad shake of his head. "It doesn't look good; he is too small. I'm surprised he's even able to breathe. I don't see how he can possibly survive. I'm sorry."

"But he is alive," Nathan insisted. "Surely, there is hope as long as he is still alive."

Peter looked deeply into his brother's eyes, as his gaze spoke words that Nathan did not want to believe.

"We'll see," he said at length.

Mrs. Layne stayed the night to help, but the babies, tired from the process of birth, slept peacefully, as did Hannah, on her stomach, until the early hours of the morning, at which time she abruptly and completely awoke. Noticing that he was not in bed with her, she carefully made her way into the front room where she found Nathan sitting quietly, still holding their little son, examining his tiny features.

"Honey, why don't you put him down and come to bed?"

"We have no place to put him, Hannah; there are only two bassinets and I'm afraid he will die in his sleep. If it must happen, then it will be in my arms."

Hannah ran her fingers through her husband's hair and settled next to him, where together they waited out the rest of the night, holding their infant son until the earliest morning's light.

Chapter Eleven

Andrew's Hope
August 1907

Peter came early the next morning and was surprised to find Hannah feeding her very much alive little son. Nathan, having seen him through the night, had finally succumbed to his exhaustion and, after letting Peter in, Mrs. Layne had resumed her business in the kitchen taking care of the household chores.

"Good morning, Peter," Hannah called cheerfully. "Have you eaten yet? I think there's still some warm breakfast in the kitchen."

"Thanks, but I didn't come for breakfast. I see the little guy is still with us. How is he doing there? Is he getting anything for his efforts?"

"It seems so," she smiled. "You know, I really think he'll be all right. He is so determined, even if he is tiny."

Peter began listening to the baby's lungs and then shook his head. "I can't give you any reason to hope for it, Hannah, though I never thought he would survive even this long. Have you named him?"

"Yes; we've decided on Nathan Andrew Layne."

"A junior?" he asked, trying to be cheerful, but feeling a burden at their obvious and complete attachment to the tiny boy. "That could get confusing," he began, and then stopped himself, realizing that they would not have the time with him long enough for it to be so.

Hannah noticed his melancholy as she kissed her little son and then raised him to her shoulder, very gently rubbing his back.

"We'll call him by his middle name. And, Peter, I think he'll be fine. You needn't be so glum."

He looked at her for a silent moment before taking a deeply burdened breath. "Hannah, you mustn't get your hopes up. It will only . . ."

"Peter," she interrupted, "we must hope. He is our son. Our hope and faith and love are all that we have to give him. Besides, I have a feeling about him. He has a determined spirit. I think it will all be fine."

"Very well. How are the girls?"

"They are wonderfully robust. Melanie hasn't completely caught on to the nursing yet, but I'm sure she'll do fine eventually, and Meredith is a ferocious eater. I have no worries about that one."

"Which is which?" he asked as he began a gentle check on them, trying not to disturb their slumber.

"Merrie is on the right, with the ribbon around her ankle. She was the first baby."

"I see; and how are you feeling, Hannah? Are they letting you get any rest?"

Hannah laughed. "I am feeling euphoric, Dr. Peter, a true state of heavenly bliss. The babies have slept almost constantly since the first couple of hours. I've had to wake them, all but Merrie, just to feed them, and even she goes right back to sleep after her hunger is satisfied."

Peter smiled at her enthusiasm. "I suppose you had better enjoy it while it lasts. I'm sure the girls will keep you busy enough in the future."

"I suppose they all will," she persisted.

"Well, I need to be getting back home. Alannah and I will be in town at the office today if you need me. Other than that, I'll bring the scales by later this afternoon so we can get an accurate weight on them."

"That would be wonderful! Thank you, Peter. Say hello to Alannah for me, will you? And thank her for her help."

"Yes, I will."

"And don't forget your honor, son," Mrs. Layne added as she came into the room.

Peter nodded as she gave him a mother's kiss. Then he was off, closing the door behind him.

Sarah settled herself into a chair with a sigh. "You know, Hannah, I hadn't thought about it before, but I left those two completely alone together last night. I hope they behaved themselves," she smiled.

"Are they very fond of each other then?"

"Well, Peter is certainly fond of her, though I haven't been able to completely figure her out yet. She seems to be somewhat interested in him, but she's quite reserved about the whole matter."

Hannah laughed. "Oh, Mother; how romantic! I wish I could be a bug in the rug over there to watch them."

Sarah smiled at the comment. "There hasn't been a whole lot to see yet, I'm afraid, besides Peter watching her as much as he can without being caught. He is so busy keeping an eye on her that he doesn't notice me in the least. I think she would probably peek at him a little more if she could get the chance. It really is rather comical; she will look up and Peter will instantly change his gaze to someplace else, trying not to look so obvious. I wonder how they handled it last night, being alone."

"Tell me more about her. How does she respond to him?"

"Usually she seems a little embarrassed," Sarah shrugged, "but lately I've seen her smile to herself over it, so she must not think it too terribly unpleasant. I can only imagine how awkward they must have felt last night though." She smiled again at the thought.

Hannah smiled too. "They sound charming."

"Well, if I were to be a 'bug in the rug' anyplace, as you say, it would be down at that office today. I think going through the births together yesterday may have lowered a few barriers for them both." Sarah settled into her thoughts once again. "I wonder how we should work this out."

Hannah, who was still tending to her tiny son, looked up. "Work what out?"

"Peter and Alannah. I was planning to stay and help for quite some time, but it would hardly be appropriate to leave the two of them alone like that night after night. She seems a very nice girl, Hannah, and don't mistake my intentions, but she has a mother's walk, and Peter is so fond of her. I'm sure they would both maintain their honor given a fair enough chance, but leaving the two of them alone in that situation night after night for the long term could only lead to a great temptation at best."

"A mother's walk? What do you mean?"

Sarah glanced over at Hannah and then off out the window, taking time to choose her discretion. "Nothing, Hannah. She really seems like a very nice girl."

"Well, just the same, I'm sure Nathan and I can handle the nights together. The harvest is nearly over. I'm sure we can do it ourselves; you needn't worry about staying."

"Oh," Sarah laughed, "you are so sure, are you? After your vast experience of less than a day at mothering," she added teasingly. "You would be lucky to get enough rest with one baby, let alone three. They don't sleep like this for very long. And then with this little boy here," she added, gently taking Andrew from her arms. "He is so precious and tiny, but neither of you will get the rest you need if you're going to be holding him all through the night."

Hannah sighed softly. "Nathan said he would do what he could today after he got some rest. I think he plans to go over to John's and see about borrowing their cradle. They're not using it at present."

"Kelly would be happy to loan it, I'm sure," Sarah agreed, "but you are going to need a lot more help than Nathan and another cradle; I can promise you that."

"Maybe Alannah would be willing to come here nights, and if not then Susannah might help, or maybe we could even send for Janette. I'm sure something will work out."

"Well, I'll stay a few nights more. Do you want me to ask Alannah then?"

"Yes, that would work. It will be an opportunity to get to know her better. What is she like at home?"

"Quiet," Sarah answered. "She doesn't start any conversations, but she seems hungry for friendship and love, though she stays cautious about getting attached to people. I think she may have had a hard life."

"I think you might be right."

Just then they heard some rather loud snoring from the bedroom.

"Heavens! What is that?"

Hannah smiled and went into the bedroom, returning as soon as the snoring had ceased.

"Those babies will never sleep through that. When did Nathan start snoring? He never did it while he was at home."

Hannah merely shrugged. "He rarely does now either, and only when he is extremely tired, which is a little more often through the harvest," she smiled. "If I rub his arm, he usually rolls over and stops. The poor man," she smiled, looking off toward the bedroom. "He never slept a wink last night, but stayed up and held little Andy the whole time, offering his prayers, I'm sure."

"He is a tiny one, dear," Sarah offered, looking at the grandson in her arms. "He can't weigh more than three pounds."

"I know; the girls feel so heavy after I've held him. They must be close to twice his weight," Hannah concluded. "But the Lord willing, Mother, he will survive."

Chapter Twelve

HANNAH MEDDLES
OCTOBER 1907

Autumn wore on through September and eventually into October, with its crisp morning air and profusion of color. As it worked out, Alannah agreed and was hired to help tend the babies two nights a week, on Tuesdays and Thursdays, with Sarah taking Mondays and Wednesdays, leaving the parents to manage on their own the remaining three nights. Even Susannah tried to help on occasion, but being the eldest of her siblings she had her hands full merely keeping up with what was needed at her own house.

The demands of three new babies were enough to exhaust them all entirely, since sleep during any night one of them was in charge was almost unheard of. Hannah had to remain "available" on all the nights for hungry infants as well, but the babies flourished, and even little Andy was growing rapidly and picking up weight. Eventually, Peter fully admitted that his prospects looked very good as well.

Nathan had wanted to send a request for Janette from the start, but Hannah was hesitant. Being woken up nights and having to stay up, many times for hours, was enough to try the patience of a seasoned adult when exhaustion was wearing on them so heavily, and Janette was still so young. She doubted whether she would have the judgment and maturity to handle such a circumstance.

The subject was debated at length until, in extreme exhaustion toward the end of September, she agreed that even if Janette could only manage one night a week it was worth the request. Sarah Layne volunteered to write the letter, sharing with the Colorado Laynes any and all news about the family. She detailed Nathan and Hannah's routine in a most in-depth manner, eventually asking if Janette might be interested and available to "help out" for a few months.

Adam Layne read the letter aloud one evening during dinner before folding it up and putting it back in the envelope. Placing it on the dining table near his plate, he patted it with a thoughtful, if not hesitant, finality.

"It sounds as if they have their hands full enough, Nanette. I wish we could help them, but it will have to be in some other way."

Janette, who up to this point had been in speechless bliss over the request for her help, instantly let out a protest.

"Oh, but Papa, you can't possibly mean you won't let me go, can you?"

"I can and I do," was his firm reply. "You have studies to tend to, and you are merely a child still, Janette, much too young for a task like that."

"But they need me, Papa; and I could carry on with my schooling there. I could go with Susie Harrison."

"Janette," her mother broke in, "you really have no idea what it would call for; you would be completely exhausted. I'm afraid your father is right. You are still very young, only sixteen."

"I'm sixteen and three quarters," she insisted. "And I could do it, I'm sure I could. They need my help. Aunt Sarah even said they could use my help if I was available."

"Well, you're not available," her father declared. "They will just have to find help somewhere else."

"Oh, but Papa . . ."

"Janette, I said no, and no is what I meant! Now, not another word about it."

Janette stood from the table and looked angrily at her father before turning and running to her room where she made no attempt to muffle the sorrow of her disappointment. Nanette read the letter to herself again while Adam perused the evening paper.

"Can you imagine what it would be like to care for three little babies? Why, feeding them alone would be a full-time job. Poor Hannah, she must be exhausted. I can't even imagine."

She looked over toward the staircase and Janette's room before looking back at the letter and finally at her husband.

"You know, Adam," she began, "maybe Janette could do it. She does have an extraordinary amount of energy and she loves babies. Maybe Nathan could have an influence on her; she nearly worships them both."

"Nanette, let's not start this, please. Janette is our baby; she is only a child."

"She's sixteen and three quarters," Nanette rejoined with a smile and a shrug. "I married you when I was barely seventeen."

Adam visibly shuddered at the thought. "But you were so much more responsible; there is no comparison. Janette is sixteen going on twelve; she thinks that life is nothing more than one big picnic. She can't even keep her room clean, let alone have the kind of judgment she needs to know how to conduct herself on her own."

"But she won't be on her own, dear; Sarah is there, and Nathan. They can watch out for her. It would only be a short while, maybe four months, or five. This may just be the opportunity she needs to teach her a little responsibility. She's never had to look out for anyone besides herself."

Adam still refused. "Nanette, the answer is no, absolutely not, and that is my final say on the matter. Now, not another word about it."

❧

"Oh, Alannah!" a very harried Hannah began, "I'm so glad you're here. Merrie and Andy have been crying for the last hour at least."

Alannah, who had stopped by on her way home from town, quickly took Meredith from one of her arms, leaving her to tend to Andrew alone.

"Where's Sarah?" she asked.

"She went home to rest and has never come back."

"She was very tired," Alannah agreed with a smile and a nod, while still trying to quiet her charge, "but where's Nathan?"

"He decided to run to town and check the mail while the babies were asleep, before they woke up."

"Well, he won't find it, I'm afraid. The postman gave it to Peter, who asked me to drop it by, since he had to make a couple of house calls before he came home."

By this time, both babies were calming down, so Alannah retrieved the stack of notices and letters. "This one says that you have a parcel to pick up from Sears and Roebuck, dated October twenty-sixth?" she laughed. "That's three weeks, Hannah. No wonder the postman delivered this to Peter."

"Oh, that will be Andy's crib," Hannah laughed to herself. "Poor Mr. Jacobs, I'll bet it has been horribly in the way in that little post office of his."

"Well, that isn't all; there are four other catalogue notices here as well. What would they be?"

"I haven't the faintest idea. Nathan must've ordered them."

"Let's see, what else is here?" she said shuffling through the stack. "Some things from the bank, and here's a letter from Colorado, from some Laynes. Cousins?" she asked, handing the letter to Hannah.

"Nathan's brother is there, but hopefully this one is from his uncle. Yes, it is. Mother wrote and asked if Janette could come and stay for a few months to help out with the babies." Hannah checked the postmark. "Fortunately, this one hasn't been gathering any dust. We were wondering when we'd hear from them."

She opened the letter and read it aloud.

Dear Hannah and Nathan,

Thank you for inviting me to stay with you and help with the babies.

Alannah laughed out loud. "Thank you? She really doesn't know what she's getting into, does she?" Hannah had to smile as she continued.

I'm sorry it has taken so long to reply, but it took us a little while to talk Papa into it. He finally gave up this morning and said I could come during winter break at school, right after Christmas, but he said I must start school there as soon as possible after the first.

"School?" Alannah responded. "How old is she?"

"Sixteen. We only wanted her to help out on Fridays, one night a week. It shouldn't interfere with her schooling."

She continued with the letter.

Caleb said he would bring me if Nathan would pay his fare as well. I'm so excited to come. I can hardly wait!

Devotedly yours, forever,

Janette Layne.

"Who is Caleb?"

"Nathan's brother who lives in Colorado. His wife is from there."

"Oh, I think I've heard a thing or two about him, come to think of it."

"What a relief; I'm so glad she's going to come."

"Will you still need me after she gets here?"

Hannah laughed. "Definitely so! Don't think you're off the hook that easily. How is it working out for you between here and the office?"

"I think it'll be all right. Peter is getting busier and there's plenty of work there, but it should work out fine."

Hannah thought she noticed a slight blush in Alannah's cheeks at the mention of it and decided to pursue the topic a little further.

"So, is Peter being good to you?" she asked with a coy smile.

Alannah absolutely flamed in embarrassment as she kept her gaze fixed on the baby in her arms and away from Hannah's eyes.

"He's been very kind," she said, her voice trailing off as if there might have been a little more on her mind.

"And . . ."

"Why isn't he married?" she asked at last, looking up at Hannah. "He is twenty-six years old, and so very kind."

"I don't think he's given it enough thought or effort in the past. He can be awfully shy around women he doesn't know well, but he is a wonderful person. I think he probably doesn't know what to say, so he'd rather not risk saying anything at all."

She thought she saw a glimmer register with Alannah, but felt she had been as nosy as she dared.

"What kinds of things does he like?" Alannah pursued.

"Well he used to be fascinated with frogs and abandoned bird nests, but I think he's probably outgrown that by now. You know, I haven't sat down and talked to him about such things for so long. I couldn't tell you for sure what his interests were nowadays, except for people in general, and possibly one very obvious one; but you'd probably know more about that than I would."

Alannah flamed again. She had come to trust Hannah in her candid honesty over the months, though she was not ready to be quite so open herself.

"If you like, I'll make it a point to find out."

Alannah didn't answer, and Hannah wondered how two people who were being so shy about it all would ever get together, even with some gentle help. She would have wondered longer, but the sound of someone in the lane changed the direction of her thoughts.

"Oh, maybe that's Nathan now," she stated hopefully, though after a few minutes, it was Peter, instead, who knocked and then came in.

"Dr. Peter, hello!"

"Hi, Hannah, Alannah."

He never once looked at Hannah, but had his attentions fairly well fixed on Alannah instead. Meanwhile, Alannah diligently kept her eyes riveted on the baby in her arms. Peter sat in a chair opposite her, though he didn't seem to have much else to say.

"So, Peter, how's business?" Hannah began, making a hopeful attempt at starting a conversation.

"Fine; busy."

"That's what I hear from Alannah." Hearing Melanie stir, she handed Andy to his uncle and retrieved her daughter from the other room. "Do you like it?" she continued.

"I like helping people. Yes, I guess I would have to say I enjoy it."

"What other things do you like? I don't think I've asked you that question since we were children."

Peter looked a little flustered. "I've been so busy; I haven't given it much thought," he shrugged. "I guess I enjoy the ocean, and swimming at Silver Falls, though I haven't given either of them much attention lately. I enjoy being around family and people I care for."

He cast another glance at Alannah who was still staring in earnest at the baby, while Hannah chose to pursue the safest of the three topics.

"What do you like best about the ocean?"

"It's so peaceful there with the waves rolling in and the meadow."

"Yes, I love the meadow," she agreed. "Have you been to the meadow yet, Alannah?"

"No, I haven't."

"Well, Peter, why haven't you shown her the meadow yet?"

Peter looked stunned as he struggled for words. "I . . . well . . . um . . ."

"Would you like to see the meadow?" she asked Alannah.

"Well, yes, I guess I would," she answered.

"There you go, Peter. You need to take a day and show her the meadow and the falls. I heard Mother say there was to be a dance coming up too, in town on Saturday. You know, Alannah, Peter is a wonderful dancer. Do you like to dance?"

"I've only been once."

"Well there you are," she concluded. "Peter, why don't you show her around on Saturday, and you could both go to the dance Saturday night."

Peter stared at Hannah in shock, acting as though he had been struck. When Hannah nodded toward Alannah and mouthed back the words, "ask her," he gathered his courage and finally spoke.

"Would you like to go?"

Alannah looked up, and even Hannah was surprised at how calm she appeared as she answered. "Yes, I think that would be nice."

About then, they heard Nathan in the lane.

"Alannah, are you in a rush, or could you help me put dinner together? Peter, would you keep an eye on the babies for us?"

Peter agreed and the two women left for the kitchen, with Hannah rather congratulating herself all the way. Saturday was only two days off and she was hoping, for Cupid's benefit, that the dry spell of the last couple of days would last through until then.

It was going to be an interesting weekend after all.

Chapter Thirteen

HELPING PETER
OCTOBER 1907

"Nathan, do you suppose we could find someone to watch the babies Saturday and drop in on the dance? We haven't been out to anything for so long. I'm beginning to forget what civilization looks like."

"Oh, Hannah, do we have to do anything? I'm so tired and we don't have anyone to help us during the weekend. We'll be so utterly exhausted."

He was, at that moment, dropping into bed in a state of extreme fatigue, closing his eyes against his exhaustion.

"Oh, honey, please, it would be so fun, and if we're careful we could get a little extra rest by then."

"I can tell you had a nap today," he said accusingly. "Otherwise, you wouldn't even suggest such a thing."

"Oh, Nathan," her tones rang out with disappointment. "I hardly remember what it's like to dance with you and have you hold me in your arms."

Laughing softly, he reached over and took her by the hand, pulling her onto the bed and into his arms. "I'll hold you while we sleep."

"Nathan . . ."

"Hannah, I don't know where you've gotten this sudden burst of energy, but I wish you'd tell me so I could tap into it too. Why don't you get the babies tonight if you're feeling so chipper? I'll sleep through for once."

"You have the easy part; you only bring them to me and put them back to bed, and you nearly do it in your sleep while I have to stay awake the whole time to feed them."

"All right, you win."

Hannah snuggled into his shoulder. "Then you'll go?"

"I didn't say that. Why are you so bent on the dance?"

"We don't have to stay the whole time."

"No?"

"Peter's taking Alannah to it."

"Really? That's good. How did he ever get up the courage to ask her?"

"I kind of helped."

"Ah, so now this is making more sense. You want to spy on them then and see how the results of your matchmaking will turn out."

"Well, yes."

"This is all making complete sense now."

"Then you'll go?"

"Absolutely not. You shouldn't interfere, Hannah."

"Then you'd better teach Peter how to carry on a conversation before Saturday morning."

"Morning? I thought you said it was Saturday night."

"Well he's taking her to see the meadow and Silver Falls in the morning."

"Obviously your doing also."

"Why do you say that?"

"Because Peter would never ask her to go on an outing like that."

"Don't you think he is capable of being romantic at all?"

Nathan pulled one eye open to look at her and then closed it again. "No."

"Don't you think he has any dreams?" she persisted.

"Yes, I'm sure he has dreamed about taking her to all of those places a hundred times over, and he would thrill to think she was in the same house while he was doing it, but I'm certain he wouldn't carry it any further."

"How did you and he turn out so differently?" she mused.

"I don't know," he was beginning to drift off to sleep and Hannah could tell that the conversation was being effectively ended.

"Nathan?"

"Hm?"

She hesitated a moment more and then began in very quiet tones. "Unless you stand up right now and tell me we're not going, then I'll assume we are."

There being no response, Hannah smiled and snuggled into his shoulder again.

❧

The following morning, Peter hastily came in through the kitchen door and sat at the table, obviously disturbed.

"Hannah, I can't take Alannah to any of those things. You've got to help me out of it."

"Nonsense, Peter," she laughed. "She wants to go with you."

"But I can't spend that much time alone on an outing with her. I wouldn't have a clue of what to say."

"Ask her questions."

"Like what?"

"Well, ask what she's interested in, or what her favorite flowers are, or where she'd like to be if she could close her eyes and be anywhere in the world."

"I can't ask her that."

"Why not?"

"It's not . . . oh . . . just tell me more things I could say." Peter was jotting down notes as they spoke.

"Well what do you want to know about her?"

"Everything."

"Like what?"

"I'd like to know about her past."

"I think that might be an unhappy topic for her."

"But I want to know still."

"Then ask her."

"How?"

"Ask her what her favorite age was and why. Ask her what her happiest memory was, or if she likes the snow or—I don't know, Peter. Don't you ever dream of going places or doing things with her?"

Peter flushed crimson, and Nathan laughed as he entered the room. "I'd say he does!"

"Well, what do you dream about? Ask her if she likes those things."

Peter winced and Nathan had to laugh again. "Maybe you'd better not, Doc."

"Well, Nathan, what would you talk about if you were out on a date with her?" he insisted impatiently.

"I wouldn't. I'm married, and I don't think Hannah would approve of my dating other women."

"You know what I mean! What did you talk to Hannah about?"

"I didn't; she did all the talking," he said, winking at Hannah.

"Oh, Nathan Layne, that isn't true at all and you know it. How is it that you've become so suddenly spry this morning? Last night you would hardly even speak to me."

"The conversation had ended."

"No it hadn't; you fell asleep before it ended."

"I answered all of your questions, didn't I? And I didn't stand up and say we weren't going, did I?"

Hannah laughed. "You heard that?"

He smiled. "And you thought I wasn't listening."

"Hannah," Peter broke in. "I need more questions."

"Why don't you ask her to marry you, Peter?" Nathan laughed. "That's a question."

"Funny, Nathan," he replied in very unamused tones.

"Okay Peter," she began, "play a getting-to-know-you sort of game. Give each other a topic and then tell each other a story about how that topic relates to your life. Nathan, do you have any suggestions, seriously?"

"Sure," he nodded, "pray about it."

Hannah was about to give him another futile look, but glancing at Peter first, she noticed that he seemed quite content with the suggestion, and so only added one last thought.

"And be honest."

Chapter Fourteen

SECRETS
NOVEMBER 1907

Peter groomed the dappled gray mare to a luster, running the comb through her white mane, making certain there were no tangles in sight. Pepper verily glistened from forelock to tail due to the lengthy attention she'd received, as every last speck of dust disappeared from her thick winter coat. The young mare had greatly enjoyed the attention, though it had gone on for such an amount of time that she'd lulled off and fallen asleep.

Peter was in no hurry to finish the job; he felt at ease and comfortable in the barn, a far cry from what he feared the rest of the day would hold. Why did his hands have to sweat so much when he was nervous? And why, oh why, had he let Hannah talk him into this! He wiped his hands against his pants again merely at the thought, then grabbed another brush and tried to locate any last possible tangles from Pepper's tail. The mare let out a contented sigh and sleepily shifted her weight to the other leg.

Finally, deciding he'd procrastinated as long as he dared, he reached for the harness straps and slipped them over the horse's shoulders. As he tightened the girth strap, the mare's eyes popped open. Taking a quick breath, she held it as long as she could, and then finally exhaled in an attempt at loosening the gear. Peter patted her neck, smiled, and then secured it one last notch.

Offering a fervent prayer, he once again pulled out the list of Hannah's suggestions, trying to commit it to memory, only to put it away again with a shake of his head. Then he continued on a little further with the hitching up process. In a very few minutes, he would be expected to carry on a conversation far beyond his realm of comfort.

Outside the barn, the morning was cool and crisp, the sun occasionally peeking out from the clouds. Finally, attaching the carriage to the harness straps, he led the mare out into the fresh air, tied her off at the post, and patted her soft back. Taking a deep breath, he then headed back to the house.

"Alannah, are you ready to go?" he called at the front door.

"Almost," she called back.

Peter was surprised. It wasn't that he was anxious to leave; on the contrary, he was nervous and restless and antsy, but he was certain he'd taken long enough in the barn that she would be waiting. Now he rather wondered how women could take so long doing . . . whatever it was that they did to get ready. When Alannah finally emerged however, Peter caught his breath at the sight. Suddenly, he was glad that she did . . . whatever it was that women do.

"You look lovely."

"Thank you," she smiled, both gratified at his pleasure and a little amused at his obvious nervousness.

They had worked in the same office and lived under the same roof, driving together to work multiple times each week for nearly four months. This, however, was an entirely different realm of exposure. It shouldn't be any different, really, but it was.

After helping her to her seat, Peter climbed in himself, at last starting the horse on their way. Hannah's last words kept ringing through his mind and he wondered how to be honest and tactful at the same time. Consequently, they drove some little distance in silence before Peter gathered enough courage to speak at all.

"Alannah, I'd really like to get to know you better, but I'm at a loss knowing exactly what to say. And to be completely honest," he laughed, "I'm kind of nervous about this whole thing. Do you think you could help me out and just tell me all about yourself?"

He glanced over long enough to see that she was smiling.

"What do you want to know?"

"Everything."

"Some of it is ugly, Peter."

"That's all right."

"Then will you tell me about you?"

"If I can think of anything to say."

"Fair enough," she announced, "as long as I can ask questions."

"All right, and if you leave anything out, I'll ask questions too," he said, wondering where the conversation would lead next.

Alannah sighed. "I like your honesty, Peter, and because of it I will tell you all that you want to know. Though I doubt you'll feel much the same about me after I do."

As the buggy rattled over the bridge and down the path flanked by the stately evergreen trees, she took a deep breath and, looking out over the countryside, began the story from her earliest memories. She told him the good and bad, both the funny and the sad, all that she could recall of the events that made up her life and experience. She didn't really share a lot of detail; no, the story of Alannah's life was told more in general themes than concise description. Still, even in the brevity, the information came through with singular clarity. She seemed to have a gift for both sharing and yet concealing all at the very same time.

When they had reached the meadow, though her story had been occasionally punctuated with humor, he was amazed overall that a child could have endured so much and still come out of it alive. While at the meadow, Alannah stoically shared some of her greatest heartbreaks. They were circumstances that Peter had never imagined she might have endured, the death of her beloved sister, being hired out to whatever frightful person would pay, and myriad other afflictions.

Considering the often terrifying ordeals, he wished he could have somehow spared her from it, somehow gone back in time to change the course of events. So much of it could have been easily prevented, if only there had been someone who cared enough to protect her.

Later in the day, after reaching Silver Falls, they had made it through most of her teenage life and finally, while sitting there before the waterfall, she told him the rest. She ended the story of her life by offering an impossibly courageous smile and saying that she thought that covered "the most of it."

"You haven't told me everything," he added a little cautiously.

"No, but I've told you most of it."

Peter looked at the falls for some time, overwhelmed by the information and debating how far he might press his luck in trying to fully understand what made up Alannah, her life, her beliefs, and her thoughts. He had long since lost his nervousness, or any thought for himself. Her life was so far beyond his experience, one that he had never considered could exist outside of a bizarre account of fiction. Still, wanting to know all that he could, he dared to venture one final question.

"What about the baby?" he asked.

A wave of pain crossed Alannah's face. "You should leave that part alone, Peter. It is too much pain."

Gathering his courage, he put his arm around her and drew her closer, as they watched the cascading water flow over the rocks.

"I'm utterly amazed you have survived as well as you have," he said. Then after a moment more he added. "I do want to know about the baby though."

The Laynes had come to represent great safety and security to Alannah, showing her that there truly was another side to the possibilities for her life. It had been all she thought she could muster merely to risk their respect and share what she had. Now, Peter was asking for the ultimate secret, the ultimate truth, which she feared might end it all. With only the warmth of his arm to buoy her courage, Alannah heaved a burdened sigh and listened to the steady cadence of the cascading water. Resting her head against his shoulder, she resigned her fate to what she hoped would be his compassion and then confessed the rest of her past.

"I had a baby when I was twenty."

"Last year?" he asked in surprise.

"Yes."

"What happened?"

"After a few weeks we both became ill; I'm not sure what from. I was so sick I couldn't sit up or even focus my eyes. They wouldn't let me see her. All I wanted was to see my baby; I begged for her. Then they said she was gone."

"She died then?"

"I don't know; they never would say. I was afraid they might have sold her. Originally, I left, determined that I would find her and make my life right. A neighbor of ours, Mrs. Stotts, very kindly loaned me the money to go without my mother's knowledge. I searched aimlessly for weeks until my wanderings brought me, penniless, to here. I've been trying to pay back Mrs. Stotts each month, and I've nearly accomplished it, but it is so much pain. I don't even know if my daughter is alive."

"What was her name?" Peter asked.

"Maggie."

"How would you know her if you found her?"

Alannah almost laughed at the utter futility of the question and shook her head. "I would hope I could remember her very scent, the light of her eyes, and her every feature, but she was so little. Babies change so much and she would be more than six months old by now. Surely, there would be almost nothing to recognize her by." She leaned back, exhausted from the emotion, and tried to clear her mind. "My poor, little Maggie," she whispered. "I have watched Hannah's babies and longed for her." At last, she concluded her thoughts. "Now, you will probably want to send me off, and I can't blame you for it."

She looked up to see Peter staring off into the waterfall. He said nothing for the longest time, only stared at the patterns in the falling water and tried to absorb all that he had been told. After a further silence, he managed a shrug.

"I started on this drive so nervous today, praying I would know what to say to the woman who has been in our home for the last several months, but who I felt I hardly knew. I feel now that I am with a close friend."

Alannah laughed a little ruefully. "Except that you've not told me a thing about yourself."

"I'm not sure there is much to tell after hearing your story. I've had an uneventful life where tragedy is involved. The worst things that have happened to me were breaking my arm when I was eight and Dad passing away last winter."

"Well, life shouldn't be all about tragedy. Tell me about him; what was he like?"

"Dad? Well, he was wonderful, inspiring, loving . . . a bit stubborn sometimes," Peter smiled at his memories, "but in the end, very kind. He would have helped anyone that needed it, never mentioning a word more about it."

"Maybe he was too good for this earth."

"This earth needs more people like him. We've all missed him sorely, especially Mother. Before she got so busy with Hannah and the babies, I would hear her cry herself to sleep each night. Nathan took it hard too; they were really very close. Then we found out Hannah was expecting and I suppose those babies have been everyone's salvation. Mother has thrown herself into them and into Hannah with such enthusiastic fervor."

Alannah nodded. "It helps to have a way to vent your grief."

They stayed a while longer in relative silence, a light mist from the falls occasionally wafting over them, before eventually deciding that it was time to wake up Pepper once again and start back.

As the buggy rattled over the twigs, leaves, and occasional pine cones in the path from the falls to home, Alannah remembered another detail she'd heard earlier and had since wondered about.

"Hannah said you used to have a mild fascination with frogs and bird nests. What can you tell me about that?"

Peter smiled. "I broke my arm trying to get a bird's nest out of a tree. It used to so intrigue me that a bird could build something like that with only a beak. It still seems nothing short of amazing. I guess I thought that if I collected enough empty nests and examined them closely, I'd be able to figure it out. But there were so many different kinds of birds with so many different kinds of nests, it was an endless quest."

"And the frogs?"

"They were just interesting," he smiled, "one of those little boy amusements, I guess. I spent hours catching them in the summer, trying to coax them to croak, and then bringing them all home, as many as I could manage. Mother would march me right back outside with strict orders to put them all right back where they came from."

Alannah laughed. "I can just hear her saying that."

Peter laughed too, and after some further small talk they at last pulled into the lane. He reflected once again over how very different their lives had been. When they had started out, he supposed he would hear the same types of idyllic tales as from his past, but Alannah's life had been frequently tragic and filled with hardship. Yet, through all that difference, he felt they had become well acquainted this day.

He helped her from the carriage and quickly unhitched the horse, hanging the harnesses and settling Pepper into her stall with a generous portion of hay. Finally, they went into the house and sat before the fire. Alannah tried in earnest to stay awake, but the warmth of the room, combined with her previous night's duties and the emotion of the day, began to overwhelm her.

"Peter, I'm so tired. I don't know that I'll be able to make it to the dance tonight. I feel as though I could sleep for days."

"There are still a couple of hours before we need to get ready. You could take a nap?"

He had expected that she would go lie down in her room and was completely surprised when instead she rested her head on his knee, falling asleep within moments. He watched her for a while and then watched the flames in the fire dance around the logs as he tried to sort through his feelings.

She no longer held the threat, or the intrigue for that matter, which had previously so consumed him. He wondered if her fears might have been founded, that possibly he didn't like her as much anymore. Yet the thought of "sending her off," as she had suggested, was out of the question. He felt familiar and comfortable with her now, even if his heart still ached over some of the gruesomeness she had shared. Under the circumstances, he felt she had endured it all so very well.

"How unfair it is," he whispered quietly to God, "that someone would take an innocent child and mangle their life, leaving them to ruin." Emotion only built inside of him as he considered it, wondering how a fair being could allow this sort of thing to happen. "Dear God," he whispered at last, "how can that be just?"

At his question, he began to feel a warm peace come over the room, a most overpowering and compelling love, as though the heavens had somehow opened and a love was pouring out to Alannah and himself. A thought burst into his mind.

"I am the master healer and I have intervened."

Peter looked over to the woman sleeping peacefully beside him, and for a moment he thought he saw a most noble, strong, and virtuous person there. For merely a moment, perhaps a fraction of a second, he thought he understood the entire plan of life, how we must each be tested, to prove to ourselves where our desires will be. He understood that some of the strongest must be tested to the limit of their strength. A feeling of profound warmth and love permeated his soul and again words came into his mind.

"I have accepted her sacrifice."

He heard no more after that, but the feeling persisted, along with an understanding that she was among the most courageous to come to this earth. Hers was not an assignment to earthly honor or glory, to stand in the limelight of what men esteem to be of great worth. Rather it was an assignment of sacrifice, a covenant to rise above her circumstances and stop a generation of evil from continuing on. She was accepted.

In his heart, Peter felt a new resolve to help her and to love her, as closely as he could to the love that he had known this day. In the end, he wondered at the vastness behind the plan of it all.

"Some of us are the saviors for generations to come," he concluded at last, in a whisper, "and maybe others of us are to save the saviors, sacrificed to the will of man. And yet, Alannah, I'm certain I am only helping the stronger of the two of us. Perhaps, in the end, when we can both see more clearly, you will be the one to help me."

Chapter Fifteen

The Long Weekend
December 1907

"I don't feel well, Auntie Hannah. I don't think I should stay. We've had the flu at our house and I think I've caught it."

There was little questioning the sincerity of Susannah's plight. She was pale and drained, and the flu was going around. But it was Friday. Alannah, who was to help the night before, had it and had canceled out. She had come on Tuesday, but had probably gotten it from Mother, who had canceled out on Monday and Wednesday because of the same complaint. Since Janette hadn't yet arrived, Susie had agreed to take an occasional Friday night until she did, and on this particular Friday she was their last hope before the weekend.

Hannah knew she should be feeling compassion for her niece. She ought to show her concern over Susie's health and help her home, or invite her in to take care of her herself, but Hannah wasn't feeling compassion just now. She was feeling fatigue and frustration, exhaustion and resentment, and finally guilt for feeling so selfish over the entire situation. Instead of putting her arm around Susie to comfort her, she wanted to scream. She almost wanted to ask her how she dared to do it when they were depending on her so desperately.

It was entirely irrational to feel this way, but Hannah was not feeling rational in the least. Rather, she was suffering from the very real effects of extreme mortal exhaustion, the kind in which the mind retreats and the vast needs of the body take over. The only blessing she could think of was that they had somehow miraculously escaped the "bug" themselves, so far.

She stood before Susannah, still in the doorway, and tried to force a reasonable response from some hidden well of integrity that she hoped still remained deep within her soul, somewhere.

"I'll get Nathan to help you home, Susie," was all she could manage. Not even "I'm sorry you're feeling so ill, Susie," or "I hope you feel better, Susie." She would have felt guiltier over it, except that she was too thankful that she had not chosen one of the other responses that had coursed through her mind only moments before.

Nathan was in the barn where he had been for what seemed like hours. Hannah enviously wondered if he worked out there at all, or whether he merely climbed into the loft and snuck a nap in the hay. Did he sleep while she remained alone to struggle with her own plight in the house, nursing babies and changing diaper after diaper after diaper, burping babies and being spit up on and then changing herself, then nursing some more and changing more diapers? When she wasn't doing more of that, she was washing out diapers and boiling them and hanging them up to dry and taking them down and washing more and hanging more and hauling the last load in, all the while holding at least one fussing baby and sometimes two, when she could manage it.

Excusing herself, she left Susannah at the house and forced one foot in front of the other the entire distance to the barn. It was hardly more than a hundred feet away, though to Hannah's weary mind it felt like miles. The door was open and as she approached, she saw Nathan leaning on a pitchfork in Chip's stall, staring vacantly off into space. She wondered if a person could sleep in that position, with their eyes open. She knew he was in as desperate a state as she.

"Nathan?"

Slowly, he turned to look at her, dark circles showing under his eyes. No other response came from him; he had simply turned his vacant stare in her direction.

"Honey, Susie is sick. Can you help her back home?"

A look of something resembling horror briefly replaced the vacancy.

"Sick? Hannah, how can she possibly be sick? She can't be sick!"

"She's sick and looks as if she needs some help home. I just got the last baby down for a nap. I'll finish up in here if you'll walk her home."

He handed her the fork, slowly trudging off to see to Susie's needs, while Hannah stood in the barn and tried to clear her mind enough to figure out which phase of cleaning he was in. It looked clean enough to her, so she spread some fresh straw and filled Chip's feed box with a goodly portion of hay. Finally untying him, she led him back into the barn. Pausing at Dolly's gate, she watched the mare chew away at her own meal, occasionally clearing her nostrils.

Hannah stared longingly at the hay box, as the memories of her relatively carefree childhood rushed back into the forefront of her thinking. Those were the days when a nap in Nollie's hay box, feeling the warm, moist breath and tickling hairs of Nollie's muzzle on her own face, would help ease even the most distressing moments.

Staring at the box, she wondered if she would fit, before reminding herself that she was a grown woman now. The hay box was small and she had three children and limitless chores in the house to look after. Sitting on a stump next to the pile of straw, she instead wondered how they would make it through the weekend. Susie had been their last hope. They had gone it alone last Friday, Saturday, Sunday, and Monday. Alannah had come on Tuesday, but that had been it. One day, all the help they'd had the entire week.

The fresh straw looked so soft to her and inviting. It almost seemed to be calling to her. "Hannah, love, you're so tired. Come, lie down in me for a moment. I'll comfort you and let you rest." It was more than she could resist. With almost no conflict of conscience, she crawled into it and anon sunk into a deep and profound sleep.

In course of time, she dreamt she was flying, soaring over the oceans and rivers and mountains, free from all cares. She could stop to rest on a cloud if she wished, a delightfully soft cloud. She could soar further up, or touch down with her toes to observe some wonder of the earth and then effortlessly lift off into the sky, escaping the weights of the world entirely. It was as she was soaring over the hills near the ocean, through the moonlight, past the cliffs and waves that she heard it first. The sound was very loud and must have been a train engine. No, surely it was the whistle, but it was so close and she wondered why a train would be in this place at all, intruding on the peace and solitude. Then, suddenly, she began to fall. Trying to regain her flight, she fell faster, spiraling down, over and over, tumbling toward the ground.

"Hannah, what are you doing? I've been worried sick over you! The babies are screaming and hungry; I had no idea where you were. Have you been here all along?"

The lantern light cast its speckled illumination across the walls and there was Nathan, looking worried and worn, shaking her with one hand while holding two screaming infants in the other arm. Off in the distance, after coming to her senses, she could hear the third in the house, screaming in near frenzy. Climbing out of the straw, she stumbled to her feet and tried to apologize. She was still too sleepy to know which direction to go and almost completely unable to keep her eyes open, so she followed her ears and Nathan's arm back to the house. It was dark outside, very dark.

"What time is it? I feel so desperate for sleep."

"It's nearly nine o'clock, Hannah, and we are both desperate for sleep. I've worried about you for hours. The babies have been crying since before eight. I had no idea where you were. I thought something must have happened."

"I'm sorry," she said again.

They were at the house now and she was quickly unbuttoning, trying to position the first baby as her husband rocked the next in his arms. Soon, she was feeding the second as Nathan burped the first, and finally she fed the third baby as her husband burped the second. Eventually, she was burping the last as the others were being settled into their cribs, falling asleep almost instantly.

"How strange," she wondered aloud, "they usually stay up a while after their evening feeding."

Nathan looked at her with an irritated mixture of utter fatigue and impatience.

"They've been crying for over an hour, Hannah; they are worn out. Come, let's go to bed and sleep while we can."

It was a suggestion she didn't care to argue and, letting their things lie where they fell, they both climbed into bed, quickly racing each other to sleep.

The babies slept well after working out their lungs so thoroughly, and the normal schedule for waking was passed by entirely, allowing their weary, sleep-deprived parents a few extra hours of complete and utter oblivion. But the triplets were not in so much of a deprived state and an hour of aerobic crying can only override an empty stomach for so long. By three in the morning, the silence was broken.

As usual, Meredith burst out first, scaring the other two from sleep and into a trio of screams. It took a few minutes to register, even then, before Hannah roused ever so slightly from her unconsciousness, but it was Nathan's job to bring them to her, one at a time, while following the basic meal routine. So she waited, grateful for the few more seconds to rest until he did. Only, Nathan wasn't waking up.

"Nathan," she nudged him sleepily, "the babies are crying." There was no response. "Nathan, you need to get them."

Still, no answer came from the mound beside her, so she rolled out of bed and stumbled to the nursery, following her ears to the loudest wail. Picking the baby up, she carried it back to bed. She could have fed them in her sleep, had it not been so crucial to save enough milk for the last. Again, she tried to wake him.

"Nathan, I'm nearly ready for the next one."

She tried nudging him a little harder as the first baby let out an enormous burp, but there was no response from her husband still. Putting the first one back in her crib, she lifted the next loudest immediately to her as she headed back to the bed. The nursing felt as though it was taking hours to accomplish and despite her efforts at nudging, her husband simply was not waking up. As she began burping the second baby, she resorted to shaking him.

"Honey, wake up."

If one can shout in a whisper then she was accomplishing it. Finally, in exasperation she shoved him hard.

"Nathan, are you dead?"

"What . . ." he mumbled.

"Oh, never mind," she whispered in frustration as the second baby bellowed out a loud belch. Placing him (at least he felt light like Andy) back in his crib, she fetched the final screamer and began the process anew. Not worrying so much about her supply of milk, she allowed herself to drift off in the quiet. When the baby fussed, she changed sides and drifted off again.

She had no idea how long it had been, but when she woke, the final baby was asleep at her breast. She knew she should wake her for burping, but Hannah was so weary that she merely set her gently on her tummy in the crib and headed to bed, hoping the bubbles would work their way out on their own. Barely making it back to the mattress, she immediately fell back to sleep.

What she didn't realize was that Melanie had nursed for nearly an hour, and besides being very full, had an enormous air bubble in her tummy which was working its way toward more vulnerable parts of her system. It took another hour before it began to have effect but somewhere around five in the morning, the babe let out a scream. Hannah was nearly delirious from exhaustion, but her husband still wasn't stirring.

"Nathan," she nudged him once more, "Nathan, wake up, please!"

"Hm . . ."

"The baby is crying, I think she needs to be burped."

There being no further action, she nudged him again. "Honey, please burp her."

"Oh, Hannah," he pleaded, half in his sleep, "it's only one. Can't you get her?"

"It's your turn, Nathan. I just fed them all, and by myself. You could at least burp one of them."

There was no movement, only the wailing of the baby in the nursery.

"Honey, she's going to wake the others. I just got them all to sleep." She nudged again. "Please, Nathan, I'm so tired. You're so much stronger than I am. What about your chivalry?"

"You had a nap," he muttered.

She thought a moment more. "You said you wanted to teach your children to pray from the time they were babies. Now would be a good time to start, don't you think?"

There was no response to her question and Melanie's crying was escalating while Hannah's patience had worn completely through. After nudging him a few more times, she planted her feet firmly against his side and shoved hard, with the effect of Nathan flying out of bed and onto the floor.

"Hannah!" he nearly shouted, getting to his feet.

"I'm sorry, Nathan. I think compassion is wearing terribly thin for us both. Take care of the baby and we'll talk about this in the morning."

Mumbling something she, thankfully, couldn't understand, he stumbled to the nursery, picked Melanie up and brought her to the bed, handing her to his wife. Not having heard even half of what she had said to him, he assumed she was merely crying to be fed, and Hannah, at last giving up hope for any further rest, took her to the front room so as not to wake the others.

By seven, Melanie had finally calmed down and fallen back to sleep, but dawn was touching the sky and the others would be waking soon. She didn't know if the effort it would take to wake up again would be worth the little bit of rest she might get. Gazing at the sleeping daughter in her arms, she knew she could never run away, though it was a tempting fantasy at times. Rather, she chose the next best thing.

Quietly, putting Melanie in her crib, Hannah dressed, put on her shoes and coat and took a very quiet walk to the top of the hill behind their home. There, she sat in the damp yellow grass, watching the sky lighten with the dawn and drinking in the solitude of a rare moment alone in a peaceful world. Eventually the sun crested the horizon and broke through a place in the clouds. Shining in bursts through the bare trees, it glowed on her face, causing her to breathe deeply and considered her life.

"Dear God in heaven," she whispered, "what is wrong with me?"

Shaking her head, she wondered at her weakness. Never before in her entire life, had she struggled so much with the mere basics of being kind and doing what was right. Qualities that used to come naturally now felt like an enormous sacrifice.

As the sun continued to envelop her, she sunk further down in the grass and looked up at the sky. Never had she been so utterly, desperately, and hopelessly exhausted. At times it felt the depravation would never end as she labored just to make it from one moment to the next. Lying there in the quiet morning, she thought back over the last year with a deep breath and a burdened sigh while a few ideas began to work their way through her mind.

Nathan had been right all those months ago. It's easy to be good when things are going well. And yet, the trial of this circumstance was immersed in so much blessing. How long had she wanted to be a mother? How desperately had she yearned for her own beautiful children?

"They are beautiful," she smiled and said aloud to no one in particular.

Drinking in the warm rays of light as the sun inched its way into the sky, her weary body felt as though it would melt into the earth. It was so utterly peaceful out here, and calm. Life would be calling to her soon, but for this one brief moment, it felt half a world and a sunrise away.

In the next, it would be time to go home.

Chapter Sixteen

Nathan's Little Nap
January 1908

The January snow drifted down in enormous flakes throughout the churchyard in quiet contrast to the storm that was raging inside. The very most faithful members of the community struggled to remain faithfully seated where they were, indoors, enduring the worst sermon that Reverend Blistroe had managed to deliver yet.

The good Reverend Johnson, having taken a new post, had left the Silver Falls congregation, which had since experienced the likes of several visiting ministers. Some of them had been quite pleasant and others, not so much. However, this last individual had eclipsed all prior dreadfulness far beyond what anyone might have dared to imagine.

Janette reflected at how effectively his name conjured up the image of festering blisters, and how his theology and sermons matched the likeness as well. Most of the members had endured it to the limit of their patience. His pulpit pounding and shouting condemnations to all sinners present was getting beyond what any faithful churchgoer should have to endure for weeks in a row. As the "minister" saw it, they would all endure an eternity in hell, while heaven had apparently carved out only enough space in its mansions above for him alone.

The Layne babies were generally farmed out among eager relatives each Sunday morning, Janette and Susannah each claiming their favorites and little Andy to be tenderly loved by all the others. It was just as well, since Hannah and Nathan, both in their utter exhaustion, would have been stretched beyond endurance to have the thundering hell-fire waken their young fry.

On the evening previous to this particular Sunday however, the babies had all suffered from stomach ailments and spent the entire night fretting their dismay. Having no help for the weekend, as usual, their parents were left with no other option than to either let them scream or to pace the floors holding them. A combination of each was what they employed, since it was nearly impossible to effectively comfort any two babies at one time.

Consequently, the youngest Laynes were content to sleep through the thundering roar that was masquerading about as a sermon. With the babies in reliable care, Nathan had settled with his arms crossed and his head dropped forward into a sound slumber at the end of the pew. Hannah, with her head on his shoulder, had also gratefully drifted off to sleep.

Peter sat next, with Alannah's hand in his own, a little ways further down the bench, wincing at the roaring accusations, while Sarah Layne resided at the end. Janette sat happily with the Harrison clan in the pew behind them and tried with all her might not to let the "thunder" intrude on the cuddling of her own prized charge. Leaning over, she whispered at last to Susannah.

"Susie, why don't you pinch Melanie so we could have an excuse to go to the quiet room?"

"I couldn't, Janette; and don't you pinch Meredith either. It would be cruel."

"Not nearly as cruel as having to listen to this."

The minister stopped to glare at the girls, who immediately offered penitent looks for their obviously mortal sin of whispering in church. It was yet another act for which they would surely be "confined to the fiery pits of the adversary for all eternity to writhe and to suffer."

Alannah was actually the first to hear it, probably because she knew it occasionally happened and was a little sensitive to the problem. She nudged Peter. When he didn't respond to her nudging, she whispered to him to nudge Nathan quickly as it was growing louder.

Peter only shook his head and, after whispering something back to her, lifted his chin in full defiance and let Nathan snore on.

Mrs. Layne was aghast when it finally became loud enough to reach the end of the pew, but neither she nor the Harrisons behind her could do anything. To get up and go over to wake Nathan would, without doubt, incur the wrathful judgment of the booming reverend and, presently, the entire congregation was trying with their might to sit as still and unnoticed as possible.

It was obvious that Peter had no intentions whatsoever of waking him, and he was the only one within arm's reach. So Nathan snored louder and louder until the racket could at last be heard over the other racket of a sermon by Blistroe, who stopped mid-sentence and turned himself fully about to face poor Nathan in his noisy, respite slumber.

"This," he boomed, while pointing a raised finger, "is exactly what I've been referring to. You there! Young man, wake up. Wake up, I say! You have no right to slumber while the devil obviously has your soul wrapped in the chains of his eternal destiny!"

His voice verily thundered through the building, and had it not previously been so thunderous, the command might have woken Nathan up. But his exhaustion was deep and one boom sounded like the next, registering not in the least in his unconsciousness. The whole room was silent with the exception of the snoring, which by now had reached a relatively deafening volume.

Alannah nudged Peter again as the entire congregation sat in nervous dread and silence. They didn't fear so much the sermon as what the reverend's maligning of Nathan's character would be. He had helped many a family in that room in one way or another from time to time, and they all knew with a surety that God would never condemn such a generous soul.

No one was at all sure where it began. Peter thought he heard it from Janette first, a nervous giggle which, when she made an attempt to squelch it, only erupted into more, spreading contagiously along the bench. They all tried not to laugh, but the room had been so tense and somehow it all seemed a little too funny to be true. The snickering spread the fastest among the children and teenagers, but when old man Henrie, who had been sitting contemptibly on the back row, let out a loud "guffaw," it was more than the rest could valiantly endure and several adults burst into fits of chortling laughter as well.

Reverend Blistroe stood for a moment in gaping astonishment before he could stand it no longer. He turned first one way and then the other, raised his finger, and opened his mouth to boom further. When nothing came out, he instead left the building for his quarters in desperate haste. No one had dared to laugh at his sermons before!

It took the congregation a full ten minutes after he left to calm down and contain themselves. Eventually, one of the elderly gentlemen stood up in front, wiping the tears of his mirth from his eyes, and offered a prayer to close the service, including a petition (after yet another squelched chuckle) for the Lord to "forgive them one and all." Finally, he dismissed the crowd to their homes.

Only after most of the people had filed out did Peter nudge his brother to wake him. Nathan obliviously rubbed his face and then woke his wife.

It was quietly determined among the relatives afterward that someone would volunteer to help out each Saturday night, this for the betterment and spiritual survival of the community as a whole.

As for Reverend Blistroe, the poor man, he packed his bags and left on the first train out of Silver Falls Monday morning, with a destination of "anywhere but here."

The board was contacted immediately and notified of the vacancy, and another minister was arranged to fill the post so abruptly abandoned. By Tuesday morning he was sent for, and by Friday night the Reverend Carlen Sanderson arrived.

Chapter Seventeen

THE NEW MINISTER
JANUARY 1908

"Hannah, love!" Nathan called from the front door, obviously excited about something.

"What is it?" she called back.

"The new minister is here. I met him in town and invited him to dinner."

Nathan was so proud of his accomplishment since half the congregation, it seemed, had turned out to welcome him in and he was immediately invited to several homes at once. Having never been to Silver Falls and not knowing one face from the next, he simply accepted Nathan's invitation because it had been offered first.

Hannah quickly began picking up things in the front room that had been scattered around throughout the day. With arms full of odds and ends, she was heading for the bedroom to stash it all when the minister walked through the front door.

"Hannah, this is Reverend Sanderson, our new minister."

Hannah turned and froze in her tracks, becoming white as a sheet while the contents in her arms fell to the floor. It was him! He had come, and he was as handsome as he had ever been, the same winning smile and penetrating eyes.

"Hannah Harrison!" he laughed in amazement. "Imagine, meeting you after all these years."

With an enormous smile, he quickly walked over to help her gather up her things from the floor.

"Thank you, Carlen," she managed quietly.

Carlen Sanderson gave another laugh and then touched her chin. "I had no idea Nathan's wife would be you, or even that you were here. Can you imagine it? After all these years. I've often wondered what became of you since you left."

In his eyes, Hannah saw the same things she had known all of those years ago and it quite unnerved her. She loved Nathan dearly and wondered how this could be happening at all.

"It appears you two know each other already," Nathan finally concluded, settling himself in a chair.

Hannah quickly excused herself and headed to the nursery to deposit her armload of clutter and attempt to gather her completely scattered wits.

Carlen took a seat, still shaking his head. "I had no idea. Can you imagine that? You're a lucky man, Nathan."

"I like to consider myself fortunate, but just how is it that you know my wife so well?"

"I had been assigned to the Mapleton post before she left. It was my first permanent position after leaving the seminary and Hannah was living there with her uncle, Jason. They were a fine family and she was the loveliest young thing I'd ever met. Lucky for you she moved here," he laughed, "or I am certain I would have married her myself. I really have wondered about her. They said she ran away and I was dumbfounded at first that she could have done such a thing, but later Jason Harrison quietly pulled me aside and told me the details. He said that, for her safety, he couldn't reveal where she was. I had no idea," he concluded, laughing once again and shaking his head. "Had I known at the time, I would have come for her."

Hannah could faintly hear the conversation from the bedroom. She knew she needed to go back in and eventually serve the supper that had been left on the stove. At this moment, however, she was wishing she could be somewhere in the vicinity of China to give herself a chance to stop shaking and calm down. The babies were sleeping and she was tempted to wake one of them to feed, thereby leaving the two men to themselves. It was nearly time for Janette to be there anyway, she reasoned, and it would give her a few more minutes. Finally, she chose little Andy, hoping he would be quiet enough not to wake the others.

Nathan appeared in the doorway to see what was taking her and was surprised to see her settled in the rocker with Andrew at her breast.

"Hannah," he whispered, "it isn't time to feed them yet. You'll get them off schedule and we'll be paying for it tonight."

The babies' "schedule" was something that Nathan clung to with his life and breath, it being one of the few things, as of late, that he felt he could depend on. At Sarah's suggestion they had started it, and now as the babies approached their fifth month, it was the only thing they had found that came even close to helping the three of them sleep part way through the night. Andrew was the only one still too small to make it comfortably.

"I'll just feed Andy," she promised, "and be out in a minute."

Nathan shook his head at her, clearly irritated. "She's feeding the baby," she heard him say. "She'll be out in a minute."

About then, Alannah came through the kitchen door, explaining that she and Janette had decided to trade a night, and was introduced to the new minister. After this, she also appeared in the doorway of the nursery.

"Hannah, you haven't eaten yet and the girls will be waking up soon. How did Andy wake up so early?"

"I woke him, to feed him," she guiltily confessed.

"You what? He'll be off schedule!" she whispered in emphatic tones, as if her life also depended on the "schedule." Hannah only wondered if her own world was destined to be so regimented from here on out.

"Do we have to live and breathe by the schedule?" she asked quietly.

"Worse. We wake and sleep by it," Alannah whispered back.

Hannah finished up soon after and the two women went to the kitchen, quickly getting dinner served. She hoped she appeared nearly back to normal, but Alannah noticed that her color was looking a little drained.

"Are you not feeling well?" she asked.

As Nathan and Carlen were just walking in, Hannah whispered that she would talk to her about it later. At the moment, they were sitting down and, after Nathan offered a prayer, Carlen looked at Andrew admiringly.

"He's a handsome little man. How old is he?"

"He'll be five months next week," Alannah volunteered.

"Has it really been five months already?" Nathan questioned. "Boy, that went fast."

"How many children do you have?" the minister asked.

"Three," said Nathan.

"Really; how old are they?"

"Almost five months," Nathan continued.

Carlen was sure he had misunderstood the question, but no one else was correcting him and Nathan was asking him about his own family.

"I'm presently alone," he said, quickly adding. "Tell me about your congregation. I hear your last minister left rather abruptly. What happened?"

"I really don't know a thing about it," Nathan shrugged. "The children had been up all night and I'm afraid I slept through his last sermon. I think something must have happened, but I haven't the faintest idea of what."

"Do you know, Hannah?" Carlen asked.

She blushed crimson before confessing, "I slept through it also."

Carlen next looked at Alannah, who was trying to fight back an enormous smile, every so often letting out a cough that sounded very much like a choked-back laugh.

"What about you?"

"I couldn't say," she managed, shaking her head and giving another of those curious coughs. Hannah looked at her suspiciously.

"You do know what happened, Alannah, don't you?"

"I really couldn't say," she declared, erupting into such a fit of giggles that she had to leave the table altogether.

Nathan wondered at it and shook his head. "I don't think I've ever seen Alannah so cheerful, love. What do you suppose is going on?"

About then Peter and Sarah walked in together.

"Hey, Nathan," Peter called. "We heard the new minister was here."

"Yes, Reverend Sanderson, this is my mother, Sarah Layne, and my younger brother Peter. Mother, where is Janette?"

"Over at the Harrison's, Nathan; where else?"

"More Harrisons?" the new reverend asked.

"Yes, Hannah's brother and his family," Nathan added. "They live across the brook, on the farm directly west of here."

"And what about the rest of you?"

"Mother, Alannah, and I live in the white house across the brook and to the south of the Harrisons'," said Peter.

"Then Alannah must be your wife."

"No, not actually," Peter hedged.

Looking at his and Sarah's fair complexion and Alannah's black hair and dark eyes, he ventured, "Your sister?"

At about this point, Sarah rescued the conversation. "Alannah works for me and keeps house, when she's not helping out here or at the office for Peter."

Just then Meredith let out a howl, which scared Melanie, who also began screaming.

"Twins?" Carlen asked.

"Triplets," Nathan replied, as Hannah handed Andrew to him and left to care for the others.

"Were you in church last Sunday?" Carlen asked the others.

"Yes," Sarah began carefully.

"Do you know about the scuffle with the last minister?"

"Scuffle?" Sarah repeated aloud, looking at Peter, who was trying to remain as sober as possible. Peter shrugged his shoulders at his mother, who deemed it as safe an answer as any and shrugged her shoulders at the reverend.

"What about you?" she asked quickly, hoping to change the subject. "Where is your family, now that you are here and they obviously aren't with you?"

"My wife died last winter; we didn't have any children," he answered.

"Oh, I'm sorry," Mrs. Layne offered. "I didn't mean to be so insensitive."

"Dad died last February," Nathan added. "It sounds like it has been a busy year of changes for us all. About Reverend Blistroe . . ."

"Was he the last minister?"

"Yes," they chimed.

"Say no more," Carlen laughed. "I've followed him before. I think I understand the problem now completely, and that lets me know exactly the message I will need for Sunday."

They chatted on a few minutes more before Alannah reappeared with Meredith and, finally, Hannah emerged several minutes later with Melanie in a hopeful attempt to finish up her own meal.

"How amazing; I've never seen triplets before," Carlen remarked. "They're adorable."

"They are cute," Alannah agreed, "but when they are really adorable is when they're sleeping through the night." The care-worn adults all laughed in general agreement.

"Hannah, why don't you let him hold Melanie?" Nathan urged.

"How do you ever tell the girls apart," he asked, as she handed the baby to him.

"They do look alike at times," Hannah agreed. "We used to tie a ribbon around Meredith's ankle, but their personalities are so like night and day. The only time it's difficult to tell now is if they're asleep. Merrie is more assertive and independent, while Melanie is quiet and passive. Andrew is sweet, but very determined. They are all three completely different in their personalities."

"It's amazing," Carlen kept repeating to himself as they continued their visit into the evening.

Finally, it was time to put the babies to bed. It was getting late and Nathan was tempted to ask the reverend to stay the night, the truth being that he was feeling much too tired to hitch up the horses and make a drive clear out to the church and back. However Sarah, sensing her son's fatigue, insisted that Reverend Sanderson stay at their house for the night, claiming it was too late to be settling him into a strange place alone and in the dark.

Hannah blew out a large sigh of relief as they left. Later, as they crawled into bed, Nathan reached over to his wife.

"I'm sorry, Hannah, I had no clue. I hope you weren't too uncomfortable with him here."

"He's a good man, Nathan, and he gives the finest sermons I've ever heard. I'm sure Silver Falls will like him."

"I like him," he replied. "He seems like a warm and decent person." He looked over at his wife, who was staring off toward the opposite wall, apparently at nothing in particular. "You never told me about him, Hannah," he ventured.

"There's not that much to tell."

"You obviously cared for him at some point, or you wouldn't have behaved as you did tonight. And he said he was certain he would have married you had you not left. How could there have been nothing to it?"

"That's not what I said," she groaned.

"Did you love him?"

Rolling over and resting her head on his chest, she listened to his heartbeat for a minute or two.

"I thought I did, Nathan. For years I thought I loved him more than anything else, but what I feel for you is love, and what I felt for him was different somehow, something akin to a very deep admiration and a spiritual attraction. It was a long time ago and there really isn't much to tell anymore," she concluded as she began to drift off to sleep.

Nathan stared at the ceiling and considered it all an hour or so more. "Why hadn't she mentioned him before?" he kept wondering to himself.

It seemed impossible that there could be so little to say.

Chapter Eighteen

ENTER PRINCE CHARMING
MARCH 1908

Reverend Sanderson was an instant success among the Silver Falls people, and Nathan began to understand what Hannah had meant by the "finest sermons." He found himself leaving church each week more inspired than he had ever felt before.

The reverend had a deep belief that there was a profound purpose to life. His sermons reflected that, as did his humble gratitude for all of life's experiences—the good and the "difficult," as he termed it. He did not believe that any trials were doomed to be bad and refused the word. Instead, he assured the congregation that adversity, taken with faith, could help all to grow and would serve for eventual good. He further believed that most people inherently wanted to do right, and he approached each individual with that certain faith in them displayed. His love for all genuinely reflected his complete devotion to God.

Knowing Hannah as he did, it didn't take Nathan long to figure out what it was she had felt for the reverend in the past. It was obvious that he had stood worthy of it. Much of the district picked up on a similar feeling as well, and by early spring there were hardly enough seats to accommodate the growing crowd.

Even the Taylors began attending, something that had not happened in years. It was on the first Sunday in March that Janette noticed Gabriel walk through the back door for the first time and settle into a pew. She nearly gasped for excitement and quickly nudged Susannah.

"Oh, Susie, look; there's Gabriel Taylor! I haven't seen him at all before now and I wondered if I'd get the chance before I had to leave."

"Maybe you could talk to him after church."

"And Papa's not here," Janette smiled ruefully. "He won't have to ask his permission at all."

Janette, who had recently celebrated her seventeenth birthday, was feeling quite capable of taking care of herself and was secretly hopeful at the prospects. Shortly before the sermon began, Gabriel at last spotted her, throwing her a smile and a wink. It left Janette in a completely euphoric state, preventing her concentration from dwelling on much of anything besides what she could possibly say to him afterwards to convince him that he really should take her for the drives she had missed out on during her previous visit.

She didn't have to spend much strength on it, since as soon as the service was over Gabriel stood at the back of the room and waited for her to make her way out.

"Hi, Janette," he ventured quietly. "What brings you to Oregon?"

"Visiting for a few months," she replied.

"Months?" he raised his eyebrows at the answer. "What about your parents?"

"They're in Colorado. I came to help Hannah."

"Ah, the triplets; I heard about those. How busy do they keep you?"

"My days to help are Fridays after school and Saturday mornings. Otherwise, I'm relatively free."

"I see," he smiled. "So, to whom do I need to seek permission now to take you driving?"

Janette lifted her chin. "I'm seventeen; I think I can speak for myself."

Gabriel extended his arm to her and escorted her through the door. "May I have the pleasure of your company then tonight, for a drive through the countryside?"

Janette readily accepted. "I'll be at Aunt Sarah's."

Gabriel winked his approval as he ran to catch his family before they left, turning at last to wave his good-byes and smile one final, dashing smile for her to remember him by for the rest of the day.

Nathan stood and observed from his pew, holding two of the babies while Hannah bundled the third. Uncle Adam would not approve, he was certain of it, and he felt more than a little responsible for Janette. His brows were knit in concern as he wondered what to do. Janette was in his mother's charge for the day, though Sarah Layne had been outside and not heard any of the conversation. He decided to wait and think it through before saying anything to his young cousin, though on the drive home he broached the subject with Hannah.

"I saw the Taylors in church today."

"Really? That's wonderful; they haven't been to church in years."

"Yes, Janette seems quite interested in Gabriel. I heard her accept to go on a drive with him tonight."

Hannah's face clouded as she turned to look at her husband. "Uncle Adam wouldn't approve, Nathan," she said at last.

"No, I don't believe he would either. But he is nearly two weeks off by mail to consult, and I thought I heard Janette tell Gabriel that she was old enough to speak for herself." Hannah winced at the comment. "What could she possibly see in him?" he asked.

She laughed a little to herself. "He is very handsome, Nathan."

"Unless you want to consider character into that," he added.

"Why is it," Hannah wondered aloud, "that we connect beauty with virtue at all? Look at Caleb. He is, even still, so handsome, and yet out of the six of you, he is . . ." she shook her head, trying to come up with words that would express her thoughts without sounding too harsh, though they failed her completely.

Nathan smiled at her tied tongue. "He is selfish and rude?"

"Well, I didn't want to use those words exactly, but yes, more or less. And yet look at Kelly. She isn't what I would think of as very attractive at all, and, well, you know what I mean."

"Yes."

"And yet she has a heart of gold and is so completely kind. It seems entirely unfair, I think. Why couldn't it be that a person's beauty was only equal to the degree of their good character?"

"Perhaps, for some people, their test in life is, at least in part, to overcome their beauty."

"What do you mean?"

"Well, as I think about Caleb, ever since we were small children I remember people singling him out and commenting about what a good-looking young man he was. A lady once told my mother. 'What a fine set of boys you have, but this one is superb.' You can imagine how that made the rest of us feel and I know it had an effect on Caleb as well. I think he started out with the same attitudes as the rest of us, and our parents treated us no differently in their fairness or love, but at school and at church and at the dances, Caleb was always being told 'you're better than the rest.' Not in so many words of course, but effectively just the same. It was as though enough people told him, that he finally started to believe it."

"Yes." Hannah nodded. She knew Caleb well enough to understand what her husband was trying to say.

"I remember the first time he ever voiced it to me," Nathan continued. "I must have been about eight, and Mother had been baking. She told us we could each have a tart before dinner. We were all so hungry, but I had told my dad I would do a particular chore and decided to finish that and eat my tart after. As I started back into the house, I saw Caleb come out with a tart. I was so hungry and somehow I knew it was mine, probably from the jam already smeared on his face," Nathan laughed. "He started eating it right in front of me. I asked him if it was mine, and when he said that it was, after he had finished the last bite, I asked him in a fit of tears why he ate it. He told me, 'because I deserve it more than you do.' When I protested, he only taunted me saying, 'going to tattle to Mommy like an ugly little baby are you, Nate?'" Nathan laughed again.

"I probably should have; I'm sure Mother never knew." Nathan shook his head. "But to have Caleb declare himself better than me, and then try to prove it by saying that I wasn't as handsome as he, well, I've never forgotten it. I remember deciding right then and there that handsome did not equal good."

"And yet look at David," Hannah interjected. "He is certainly handsome, and he is also certainly good."

"And look at Reverend Sanderson," Nathan added. "I've heard the women talk of how handsome he is, and yet he is also one of the finest men I've ever known. I don't think he is vain at all."

"He's more than handsome," Hannah said thoughtfully. "It's almost as if he glows with goodness."

"Countenance," Nathan agreed.

"I guess, then," she mused, "people really can be as beautiful on the outside as on the inside, or as ugly, if you go by their countenance."

"Yes, but how do we explain that to Janette?" he wondered.

Hannah looked doubtful. "It still isn't very obvious, is it, except in the extremes?"

Nathan looked off down the road, obviously worried. "I wonder if we made a mistake, love, by asking Janette to come. I really don't know what to do now."

"She's a Layne, Nathan. Surely, she will choose right from wrong."

"Caleb is also a Layne, my love, and Reverend Blistroe was a minister and Gabriel Taylor has proven his intentions before, handsome though he may be. We certainly can't claim virtue by our name or position or looks alone. We can talk to Janette, but she will have to decide within herself what she will choose to be. We can only hope and pray that in the end she will not be blinded in her choices."

"If it could all just be a little more obvious," Hannah reflected, "and if we could only have more experience and wisdom in our youth. But it seems that it is folly which often brings the wisdom. We can only hope. . ." her voice trailed off as the carriage drove down the road. "If only wisdom could always come without quite so much folly attending it."

Chapter Nineteen

THE LETTER
MARCH 1908

"Oh, Susie!" Janette exclaimed in passionate rapture. "He is such a dream."

"Well, what happened? For heaven's sake, tell me."

Janette fell backwards onto the bed with her hands clasped to her heart. "I am in love, Susie; I'm sure of it. I've never felt this way before."

"Love?" Susannah asked, quite in shock. "But Janette, you've only been on one drive with him."

"But we were partners at the folk dance festival, so actually I've known him over one and a half years. My mother and father only knew each other a year before they got married."

"Married?"

"Well, of course he hasn't asked me yet. Oh, but Susie, I'm sure he will, and when he kissed me . . ."

"Kissed?" Susannah was nearly in shock, but Janette closed her eyes, very much savoring every lingering memory of feeling.

"Oh, Susie, it was like, like. . . oh!" she sighed. "It was like electricity! My whole body tingled and when. . ." Janette paused. "Well, I don't want to tell all, but I know that it must be love."

Susannah was very doubtful, but Janette seemed so absolutely happy, and besides, Susie was feeling quite intrigued with the details.

"What did you do, Janette; did you tell him that you . . . loved him?" she asked, feeling very awkward at the words.

"No, but I want to. He nearly told me he loved me."

Susie raised her eyebrows in surprise. "Well, what did he say? Tell me; I'm dying to know!"

"Well, he said I was beautiful and that he had always dreamed of meeting a girl like me and that he couldn't help but think about me from the moment he saw me. What were the words he used? Oh, yes, that his heart and mind were consumed with me."

Susannah giggled excitedly. "This sounds serious, Janette."

Janette looked over at her friend and let out a deeply passionate sigh. "I've got to tell him how I feel, Susie, I absolutely must or else I think I will burst!"

"When are you going driving with him again?"

Janette sat up, looking suddenly solemn. "I can't," she said in very irritated tones.

"Why not?"

"Because Aunt Sarah forbid it and said she would send me home in a minute if I did, simply because we were a little late getting back. Can you imagine? She sat at the kitchen table and waited the entire time, and Nathan was there too."

"How late?"

Janette gave a guilty glance toward her friend. "It was late," was all she would say.

"What did he tell Mrs. Layne?"

"He didn't have a chance. She was so upset that as soon as he helped me out of the buggy she started asking where we'd been and scared him right off. That's why I must let him know of my feelings."

Susannah looked doubtful. "I don't know, Janette. Are you sure this is right?"

Janette only sighed. "It must be. I've never felt like this before. I know it must be love and oh, Susie, I can't lose him, not now."

Susannah was still doubtful, but Janette seemed so certain that she figured she must know what she was talking about. It was, after all, an exciting thought.

"Maybe you should write him a letter."

"Yes, I think I'll do that . . . right now! Susie, where is some paper?"

The paper was retrieved and Janette began. "'Dear Gabriel . . .' Oh, no; this isn't right at all. 'My dearest love, Gabriel,'" she mused.

Susannah raised her eyebrows in surprise and giggled. "Are you sure, Janette?"

"Well, I want to tell him exactly how I feel."

"But what if someone else gets hold of the letter?"

Janette winced. "That could be disastrous. Maybe I should write it in some sort of secret code."

"But then he couldn't read it either."

Janette began to laugh. "Oh Susie, that would be perfect; then I could tell him exactly how I felt and I wouldn't need to be embarrassed at all. Only, what could I use for a code?"

"What about that Egyptian alphabet Mr. Thatcher showed us in school last week? It would be perfect."

"Yes, it would," Janette sighed, "but it was erased off the board days ago."

"I wrote it down," Susannah announced, as both girls erupted in giggles.

"Susie, you're a peach!"

The alphabet was retrieved, and Janette composed a most explicit and passionately expressive letter to the supposed man of her dreams. Feeling quite safe within the realms of a secret code, she included a few choice thoughts at the end which she refused to let even Susie see.

"What if he cracks the code?" Susannah asked, worried at the implications if ever he found out.

"However could he?" she asked. "Mr. Thatcher erased the board, and besides, no one in his family goes to school there. I'd never even heard of an Egyptian alphabet before, I'm sure he hasn't either," she ended confidently. "He'll never know."

"Then how will you ever let him know how you feel?"

"I'll tell him when the right time comes up."

"But when will you see him again? He lives clear on the other side of town."

"I'm sure he'll be at church again Sunday. I'll give him the letter then."

The entire week passed so slowly for Janette that it was painful. She had hoped that Gabriel might try to see her before Sunday, though she figured he probably wouldn't risk Aunt Sarah's wrath.

Eventually, the week inched its way along until Sunday finally arrived, leaving Janette almost ill with butterflies at the prospect of seeing him again, and in church even. It all seemed "holy" enough.

Her little quest didn't prove as easy as she thought, since Aunt Sarah wasn't about to let her out of arms reach with Gabriel in the same vicinity. Add to that the fact that Gabriel would hardly look at her with Aunt Sarah standing guard on his glances. It wasn't until after church that Janette managed to slip away and meet with him behind the building.

"I had to see you, Gabriel, and give you my thanks for the wonderful ride last week." Gabriel, who had appeared a bit nervous, relaxed considerably at her words. "I have to go," she continued quickly, "but here, I want you to have this."

She handed him the sealed envelope and left quickly, appearing back at Sarah's side nearly before she was missed. She watched Gabriel's family leave down the road a few minutes later and saw him wave, tucking the letter into the inside pocket of his coat.

"It's done," she thought to herself, feeling quite satisfied. "Even if he can't read it, he'll have to know it means something."

On Monday afternoon, as the clouds rolled in overhead and the children were piling out of the schoolhouse to go home, Susannah was feeling overwhelmed. There were shouts of glee and anticipation while some of the younger boys chased a girl down the road, tossing pinecones and pebbles at her, generally teasing her into misery.

"How immature," Janette remarked in superior tones, though Susannah was too swallowed up in her own cares to respond.

"Oh, Janette, I don't think I'll ever understand that new math, and he said he was going to test us on it Friday."

"What's so hard about it?" she asked.

"How do you mix letters and numbers? It doesn't make a bit of sense."

"Sure it does. The letter is there to stand as a symbol for the missing number, that's all. It's kind of like a blank, but when you have more than one unknown to a problem you can't just assign random blanks to each, so you assign a letter. It makes it easier to figure out that way."

Susannah looked at her, clearly discouraged, and then shook her head. "It doesn't make a bit of sense to me. How could a letter ever equal a number?"

Janette laughed. "No Susie, it doesn't equal it, it . . ."

"Janette." They heard a voice call from behind as both girls, startled, wheeled around to face Gabriel Taylor holding his horse at the edge of the woods behind them.

"I'll catch up with you," Janette whispered.

She left Susannah standing a little dumbfounded, watching them walk a ways off and stop. Susie was feeling a bit intruded upon since, after all, Janette was her friend and it was an unspoken rule that they always reserved their walks home solely for each other. She turned and walked away, very slowly, nearly the entire rest of the distance home by herself, until at the very last, when she heard a horse galloping up behind her. She watched Gabriel take Janette's hand, kissing her a last time, before helping her swing down from the back.

Susie quickly turned back, deeply embarrassed at the sight, and continued on her way as her friend ran breathlessly up behind. Janette didn't miss a beat, but resumed the conversation where they had left off.

"Now, about the letters standing as symbols . . ."

"I'm not interested in math," Susannah broke in. "I think I just want to be alone."

Turning into the Harrison lane, she ran home the rest of the distance, going straight to her room, where she cried out her sorrow across the bed. Laurel heard her distress and came to see what was wrong, but Susannah maintained her silence. After all, it was an unfounded thought. It was only one day. Still, she felt as if she was losing her best friend, "forever," as that friend always said.

Gabriel showed again the following day, and the day after that and the next after that. At first, Janette was careful to catch up, but by Friday it became obvious that their walks home didn't matter anymore.

"Janette," he called, as the girls walked down the road, early in the next week.

Janette didn't even say good-bye to Susie, but turned and left her to her own as she ran back to meet the handsome young man calling to her from the edge of the woods.

"Janette," he exclaimed, kissing her passionately, "did you really mean it?"

"Mean what?" she asked, looking confused.

"Your letter." Gabriel was gazing earnestly into her eyes, as he pulled the letter from his pocket.

"Why, yes," she laughed, "but don't ask me to translate it for you, for I won't."

Gabriel smiled as he began walking with her down the road. Susannah was still walking dolefully ahead of them within earshot, so they slowed their pace even further.

"Why won't you tell me what it says?" he whispered.

"Too embarrassing!" she whispered back.

"So it's embarrassing, is it?" he teased.

"Yes it is, Gabriel Taylor; but I meant every word of it."

Gabriel laughed. "Good," he said, "I feel the same toward you and I felt those same things that night we went driving."

Janette stopped cold in her tracks, trying to figure out if he was bluffing and had guessed it, or if he had really been able to crack the code. She took the letter from his hand and opened it to see each word translated above the code, letter by letter.

"You cracked it!" she choked.

"Yes, and it wasn't easy, I can assure you . . . at least not at first," he winked. "I thought about it nearly the whole week. Then last night it dawned on me. I figured out my name from the first line and with your 'love, Janette' from the end, that gave me twelve letters of the alphabet. I finally took a guess at what the rest of the first three words might be and that gave me four more letters. The rest was only a matter of figuring, but with so many letters as clues, it wasn't too difficult in the end. It was extremely romantic of you and I'm glad you meant it. I slept with it under my pillow all night," he smiled teasingly.

"Oh?" was all she could manage.

"Yes, and now that we know how we feel, I must be able to see you more, Janette . . . in private, not along the road."

"I don't know how," she mused aloud.

"Isn't there some place or time that your aunt isn't around?"

Janette shrugged. "She helps Nathan and Hannah on Tuesday and Thursday nights. She stays the night there, but Peter and Alannah are still at home."

"Do they stay up late?"

"Not usually, especially not on those nights. Alannah is always tired after the nights she helps out, and Peter would rather go to bed himself than not have her there to talk to."

"I'll meet you at that time then, after they've both gone to sleep. I'll be waiting for you outside."

Janette swallowed hard, but he, handsome as he was, took her fully into his arms and gave her a completely passionate kiss before he left. Eventually, he rode his horse off down the road in the opposite direction.

She felt dazed by it all, even a little nervous and confused, but she wanted to see him alone again too, and there appeared to be no other way. She could still see Susannah off in the distance and ran to catch up, at last apologizing and promising to walk with her again, "forever."

Chapter Twenty

THE LAYNE HURRICANE
APRIL 1908

"I think with those decisions made we can adjourn the meeting," Mark stated, while the Layne brothers gathered their papers and George checked with the secretary on a few incidentals in the minutes.

Nathan sat at the table, handsome and distinguished in his suit, staring a little blankly out the window of the meeting chamber. Mark and George, who had the main responsibilities of running the bank, had called a meeting to iron out a few problems and it was where they had been for the last several hours, discussing solutions as well as precautionary measures for the future.

Outside it was relatively warm and dry, with a gentle breeze blowing up from the south. After the long, wet months of winter, the change was most welcome, and everywhere a profusion of lilacs, tulips, and other similar flowers were bursting out in a glorious scene over the countryside.

Mark noticed his brother's vacant stare. "Is there something interesting out there, Nathan?"

"Hm?"

"You've been staring out the window for some time now. I wondered what was so interesting out there."

Nathan shook his head and then rubbed his face. "I'm sorry," he began a little absently. "I didn't realize I was looking out the window at all."

Mark laughed. "Deep in thought, are we?"

Running his hands through his hair, Nathan sat back in the chair. "It feels so good to be in here. There are no disasters or catastrophes happening, no babies crying, no household or farm cares. The drive here was peaceful and relaxing and outside it is so wonderfully warm."

"It sounds as if the home life is getting to you," he laughed. "I know our twins were at least twice the work as any of the others."

"Then triplets must be twice the work of twins," Nathan mused.

Mark only laughed again, "Maybe so. You ought to get out more. We could really use your help here at the bank."

"It's a nice thought," he smiled. "Very tempting."

"Well, think about it and let me know." Mark gathered up the last of his papers and left with a wave as Nathan sat alone.

Pulling out his watch, he found it was already after four, nearing four-thirty. If he left now, it would be five o'clock before he made it home. However, he just couldn't pry himself away from the soft chair in this very quiet room.

His thoughts turned to Hannah and their marriage, how there was so little romance left in it. He wondered if she even loved him anymore. The babies, it seemed, were all either of them had time for. And what about Reverend Sanderson? Nathan shook his head. He knew that neither of them would consider it, but he also realized that Hannah had loved him before and he wondered if, possibly, she did again now. He was truly an inspiring man, certainly worthy of anyone's respect.

Nathan sat a few minutes more in the peaceful solitude before his conscience got the better of him and he started on his way. Hannah had been alone with the babies since morning and he knew she would be anxious for help to return.

❧

Hearing the carriage in the lane, Hannah sat slumped on the floor with her knees pulled up against her chest, her back against the couch, staring blankly at the clock across the room. Much of her hair had long since worked its way or been pulled out of her braid from the night before. Her pajamas, which she was still clad in, had a suspicious scent of sour milk and were decorated with strained food in tiny smeared handprints here and there.

Melanie had her hands full of her mother's hair and was pulling herself to her knees by it when Nathan walked in. Handsome, groomed, and clean, he was returning after what Hannah dreamed was a relaxing break among other adults. As Melanie saw her father come through the door, she dropped to the floor, taking several strands of her mother's hair with her, and crawled eagerly across the room.

Hannah slowly moved her vacant gaze from the clock toward her husband and said nothing, but stared helplessly at his face for a moment or two before tears began to trickle down her cheeks.

Nathan stood still, the babies crawling around his feet, and gazed at his wife, quite unsure of what he should say. To ask what the matter was would be useless; however, there was something else in her eyes that tugged at his heart.

"Hi, love," he began cautiously. "Are you all right?"

Unable to speak, Hannah instead drew a deep, staggered breath as she bit her lower lip. Turning her quivering chin away to look someplace else, a fresh flood of tears washed down her cheeks.

"Oh, Hannah," he exclaimed as he tried to walk toward her.

Unfortunately, the triplets, seeing fresh entertainment enter the house, were clinging to his legs and pulling at the laces of his shoes. Shaking them loose as gently as he could, he crossed the room and helped her onto the couch, sitting down next to her and holding her in his arms.

"What's that smell?" he sniffed.

"Andy spit up on me," she whispered, attempting to choke back her sorrow. Grimacing, he changed his seat to her other side.

By then the children had made it to the couch and were clambering about their parents' legs. Meredith proudly pulled herself up to Hannah's knee, sneezed, and quickly wiped her face on the first available surface.

"Meredith! Don't wipe your nose on your mother," he began, but Hannah held up her hand to stop him.

"It's all right," she whispered, "everyone else does."

"It's not all right, Hannah. You've got to pull yourself together." She looked into his eyes briefly before her chin began to quiver again. "Are you sick, love?" he asked.

"I prayed for this, Nathan," she sobbed at last. "Do you remember how hard I prayed for this, to be a mother? Do you remember when it was only the two of us, alone, and we wanted so much to be parents?"

"It does seem a lifetime ago," he agreed.

"And, Nathan, do you remember how beautiful I used to be? I never thought I was very pretty before, but compared to this . . ." She looked down at her body and buried her face in her hands. "I feel like a secondhand Guernsey cow, with an over stretched udder."

"Oh, Hannah," was all he could manage. He wanted to say more, but the words failed him.

"And do you remember," she sobbed, "what my body used to look like, before it was stretched beyond redemption and before my stomach looked like a bowl full of Christmas gelatin?" she added, poking at it as she cried. "Nothing will ever be the same, I'm afraid, and oh, Nathan!" she exclaimed in her sadness. "You are still so handsome. You can't possibly love me anymore and that is the very saddest part of it all. I can't expect you to. I don't even think I love myself anymore. I feel so depressed."

"You are depressed, Hannah, and you're exhausted."

She lifted her chin and shook her head. "No. Don't try to tell me it will be better in the morning. I don't believe it will. It isn't even night yet."

"I wasn't going to say that."

"Nathan, you can't possibly love me anymore and if you want to leave me . . . I will understand." At this, she buried her face in his shoulder and sobbed out her agony of heart.

He didn't say anything for the longest time, only held her and surveyed the front room, trying to imagine what her day must have been like. The room had been barricaded to keep the babies contained in one place, and it looked as though a small tornado had swept around it, effectively scattering toys and books and magazines. All of the contents from her sewing basket were strewn across the floor, as well as the pages of music from inside the piano bench. There was torn paper everywhere and Nathan could only wonder to which books they belonged, hoping that none of them had been borrowed. In short, everything that could possibly be reached from a three-foot level and below had been gathered and trashed and lay quite effectively scattered across the entire room.

"Hannah, what if it had been me, instead of you?" he began, as a flash of inspiration came to him. "What if I had been the one confined to bed and struggling through a trying and miserable pregnancy? What if it was my body that had been sacrificed to bring these three little children into the world, and what if it had been me who had endured this today? Would you want to leave me, Hannah? Would you not love me anymore?" She shook her head slightly, still crying into his shoulder. "You can't know how much I love you and how much my admiration and respect for you has grown. Oh, Hannah, I don't know that it will all be better by tomorrow, but it will get better eventually; I'm sure of it."

He stood, pulling her up as well, and then guided her out of the room. "Why don't you take a bath," he offered, "and wash your hair. Put some fresh clothes on. It's beautiful outside, love. Maybe you could take a walk over to David's or John's house and visit for a little while. I'll take care of things here; and where is Janette? Isn't this her day to help out?"

"She's never shown up," she said, slowly turning to look back at the room. "And I can't blame her. If you were seventeen, would you want to leave your friends to come into this?"

"That's all beside the point," he rebutted, helping her over the barricade and into the bathroom where he started the water to the tub. He would like to have stayed to console her further, but having lost their entertainment, the babies were screaming in the front room.

Upon reaching the children, he decided that they had been given their way long enough for one day. Gathering them one by one, he placed each in their crib with a few toys while he assessed where to even begin in cleaning up. They screamed, of course, for several minutes, before eventually giving up and deciding to be content with what they had. In the meantime, Nathan hurriedly tried to restore the room, wondering all along where Janette could possibly be.

"This has gone far enough," he kept muttering to himself.

After a while he emerged back into the bathroom where he took a seat on a small step stool near the tub. Hannah was very still in her exhaustion, her face buried in the crook of her arm over the edge of the tub.

"What would you say," he began, "if we made arrangements once a week, not just to survive as we have been, but to do something fun? What if we got away for a few hours, just the two of us, to do anything we might want, anything at all?"

Slowly, she raised her eyes to face him with an expression of mixed hope and question.

"And another thing," he continued, "the babies are eight months old and plenty big enough to sleep through the night. You needn't be such a slave to them, Hannah. I really think this has gone on long enough."

"But they would cry, Nathan. I couldn't just let them cry; I couldn't bear it."

"Well, I can and I will. They are plenty big enough. Even Andrew has nearly caught up to the girls. We'll start tonight for the children and tomorrow night for us."

She was too exhausted to argue; besides it sounded too wonderful of an idea, if it could possibly work. As she closed her eyes, she could only smile at the thought, fantasy though it seemed, and hope that Nathan would come off victor in the upcoming battle of wills that was sure to test the very foundation of his patience and stamina.

"All right, Nathan," she whispered at last. With a tone of hope to her voice, she added. "And may the best man win."

Chapter Twenty-One

EVENING IN THE MEADOW
APRIL 1908

Alannah sat at her desk and checked the balance in her bank account once again. One hundred twenty-eight dollars and seventy-seven cents. That was minus the final twenty dollars she had mailed to Mrs. Stotts. Knitting her brows, she sighed. She had never planned to stay in Silver Falls for so long, yet how long would she be able to survive on barely more than a hundred dollars? And what would she do once it was gone?

She thought about the source of that money. Hannah still needed her help, especially now that it was nearing spring planting. Another month and the ground would be dry enough to be worked. Mrs. Layne appreciated her help at home, but she could manage fine now without her. Peter could always find someone else to cover her job.

Alannah rested her head in her arm and ached. It was no longer merely the job. She knew Peter loved her. To leave the job was of very little consequence, but to leave Peter? She loved him too much to be serious about considering it. Sitting back up, she tried to think through her confusion.

"Pull yourself together, Alannah," she whispered to herself. "You can't marry him. You could never marry him. You would never be the kind of person he needs for a wife. A doctor's wife?" she shook her head. "But how can I leave him?" she thought again to herself. "And yet, how can I stay? And what about Maggie? She's a year old, or will be tomorrow . . . if she's alive."

She lifted her head and looked out the window and across the town to the bank. "One hundred and twenty-eight dollars," she whispered again to herself. How far would it take her?

"It's a foolish thought," she told herself. "Maggie is surely dead and you need to accept it and move on with your life. But what if she isn't?" the other side of her argued. "What if she is alive?"

Alannah closed her eyes against the thought. If there was only some way to know. Her ponderings were interrupted by the sound of the door opening as Peter came out from the examining room, talking to Mrs. Thomas and her son.

"I think his leg will be fine from here on out. No more jumping out of the hay mow, young man, understand?" he admonished, tousling the boys hair.

As they turned and left the office, Peter stretched full, then rubbed his arm and laughed. "Boy, that little guy can pack a punch."

"Punch?" Alannah asked, turning to look at him.

Peter laughed. "He was afraid I'd hurt his leg and wouldn't let me examine it; so I told him he could hit me in the arm if I hurt him. You should have seen his eyes light up; I knew I was in trouble," he laughed again. "I was careful, too; I'm sure I didn't hurt him, but I think he rather had his heart set on the offer. I'll know not to do that again." Coming over to Alannah he began rubbing her shoulders. "What about you, lady?" he asked. "Ready to call it a day?"

She leaned her cheek against his hand, savoring the feeling of his touch. "I have a few more entries," she said at last, "and then I'll be done."

"Remind me to give you a raise," he smiled. "I wouldn't want to lose such good help."

Alannah winced at the comment, though Peter didn't notice. He was heading off to put his things away and straighten up the back room.

Peter was generally good-natured, but today he was especially spry. It was, after all, a beautiful warm spring day and things were going well for him. After finishing their work, they locked up the office and started home.

Instead of crossing the bridge as they usually did, however, Peter took the road to the west.

"Where are we going?" she asked.

"I wanted to show you something," he answered with a smile. "And don't ask me what. It's a surprise."

She noticed a gleam in his eye and figured he had something up his sleeve, but she also knew it would be useless to ask further. He had done this before, many times. Usually, it was a new dress from Miss Bailey or sometimes a hat. Peter especially loved buying her the dresses and insisted each time that she model them extensively once they were home. At that point, he would declare her too lovely to be confined to the four walls of the house and would take her off to one place or another.

Alannah often wondered which came first, the dress for the event or the event for the dress. Either way, she had more dresses already than she could ever need. She couldn't imagine why he would be buying her another. As the carriage rambled on, she could see Miss Bailey's house just up the road and was feeling pretty sure of their destination, when Peter turned the horse to the right and started down a narrow path.

"The meadow?" she asked.

Peter only smiled, continuing on to the end of the narrow road. At last they stopped. Peter locked the carriage brake and helped her from her seat. Putting an arm around her shoulder, they walked to the cliffs overlooking the ocean, where they stood, watching the sun sparkle on the water and listening to the waves crash on the rocks below.

The meadow was so secluded that it seemed they could have been alone on the earth as well as anything else. Alannah felt self-conscious about it in town where they might be seen, but here in the meadow, Peter could hold her hand or put his arms around her waist or kiss her on the cheek if he wished, and Alannah would freely respond. Anywhere else, she could not feel as comfortable. On this particular day, however, she didn't have any idea as to what might come next.

"I bought you something," he offered.

Alannah laughed. "Are we yet going out to Miss Bailey's?"

Peter smiled and shook his head. Pulling out a small box from his pocket, he handed it to her. Alannah opened it and found a delicate gold chain with a large diamond pendant hanging from the middle.

"Peter, this is beautiful," she whispered, "only . . ."

He put his fingers to her lips. "Actually it's a matched set," he announced.

Taking the necklace from the box, he fastened it around her neck from behind, leaving her to wonder at what sort of a "matched set" it could possibly be. Finally, turning her around to admire the effect of the necklace against her throat, he sat down in the grass and pulled her down to sit next to him. Taking another small box from his pocket, he opened it up, removed the ring from inside, and placed it on Alannah's finger. Lying back on the grass, he casually rested his hands behind his head.

Alannah had to smile. "Peter, I can't marry you."

"Presumptuous, aren't we?" he smiled back. "I haven't even asked you."

"Well, are you going to?"

"No."

Alannah looked at him in some confusion before looking off toward the ocean. Finally, she relaxed back into the grass beside him. He still had that gleam in his eye, she had seen it afresh, but he wasn't volunteering any further information.

"You've put a diamond ring on my finger," she began, "but you're not going to ask me to marry you. Is that right?"

"Yes, that's right."

"I'm afraid I don't understand."

"What don't you understand about it?" he asked, looking off at the sky in a completely relaxed attitude.

"Why would you give me a ring like this without any intention of asking me to marry you?"

"Why should I ask? You'll only tell me no."

She laughed and held up her hand, admiring the way the sun sparkled through the gem.

"I can't marry you, Peter; but it is a lovely ring."

"Yes it is, isn't it? Tell me, would you marry me if I were a drunkard who promised to beat you every night?"

Alannah laughed again and snuggled a little closer. "Probably not."

Peter laughed too. "Only probably," he declared. "Then I see I'd have a better chance if I were to take up drinking." He smiled before growing more serious. "I love you, Alannah, and I know that you love me as well."

"Confident, aren't we?" she retorted.

"Yes, actually."

"This is a far cry from the man who brought me to this meadow last fall."

Peter smiled. "We've lived in the same house and worked together for the last nine months. I know you through to your soul, Alannah, and I am completely, entirely, and irrevocably in love with you . . . but that's not all. I also know that in your soul of souls you want to marry me too."

Alannah became solemn. "Peter, I can't marry you; I am nothing."

"You are everything to me," he returned. "I know you're concerned about your past, but I'm the only person that knows anything about it. You needn't worry."

"Someone would find out."

"And so what if they did?"

She was quiet again for a long time. "What about Maggie?" she asked, gazing off at the horizon.

"I've thought about it at length. You haven't mentioned her for months, but if I guess right, like any good mother, you won't be able to rest until you've found her."

"I'm not a good mother," she declared in bitter tones.

"Only because you never had the chance to be," he added firmly. "If I remember right, tomorrow is her birthday. I'd be willing to do whatever it takes to find her. Once we do, we could move to another town if you like, if it would be too uncomfortable to stay here."

"Tomorrow is her birthday . . . her first birthday. I've missed nearly the entire first year of her life, if she is still alive."

"I'm certain she is."

"How can you be so sure?"

"They wouldn't have passed up the opportunity to tell you if she wasn't. We'll find her, Alannah, but we will do it together. I can't let you go alone."

"I still can't tell you yes."

"There's no need to; I still haven't asked. I did talk to Reverend Sanderson though and he assured me he would be free sometime in June, right before my vacation."

"Doctors get vacations?" she teased.

"I don't think anyone would grudge even a doctor of a honeymoon. Besides, I've made arrangements with someone else to cover for me. It's all set, Alannah. You needn't spend your strength saying yes, only to say 'I do.' "

Chapter Twenty-Two

GROWING PAINS
MAY 1908

"Oh, honey, I've forgotten my purse; we need to go back."

Nathan pulled the horse to a stop and let out a reluctant sigh. They had finally made it out of the house after every conceivable delay, and were halfway down the lane to the road. The last thing he wanted to do was go back.

"Hannah, are you sure you need it? If we go back the children will be crying for you and it will be another hour before we can get away. We're already getting past the dinner hour and we haven't even begun on our way to Amber Glen. It is over half an hour's drive. Let's just go and forget the purse."

"Don't be silly, Nathan; I made it just for tonight. Janette and Susie should have the babies in the tub by now. No one will even know that I'm there."

Reluctantly, he turned the horse around and they started back. Hannah felt a little ridiculous sneaking into her own house, but her beaded accoutrement was lying on the bed and she thought she could grab it quickly and leave before anyone might guess at her presence.

As she came into the front room, she could hear splashing and Meredith's enthusiastic squeals of delight. She could also hear the girls talking quietly but didn't concern herself over the conversation. Instead, she grabbed the purse and started quietly for the door when a certain sentence caught her ear.

"I'm going to marry him, Susie."

"Janette, you're only seventeen; you can't do that. You know your father will never give his consent."

"I'm not going to ask him," she said defiantly. "Gabriel has found someone who will marry us, and we're going to get married as soon as school is out."

Hannah stood frozen in her tracks, unable to believe her ears. They thought that the issue of Gabriel was closed months ago, yet now she was saying she was going to marry him? Maybe they were joking, or fantasizing, though Susannah's voice was frantic.

"You can't do it, Janette! What about your honor to your parents? It would be breaking the commandments."

"My honor to my husband-to-be is what matters more. He's asked me and I've given my word to him."

"Oh, Janette!" Susannah was crying. "Please, don't do this. At least talk to someone first."

It became very quiet, with the exception of the splashing, and Hannah, feeling as though her heart was sitting in her throat, felt scarcely able to breathe.

"Maybe we ought to talk about something else," she heard Janette say at last. "I thought you would be happy for me."

Hurrying quietly out of the house, she climbed back into the carriage and tried to sort out what she had just heard.

"Maybe they weren't saying what I thought they said," she wondered to herself as they made their way down the drive and started once again toward Amber Glen.

"What's the matter, love; were you found out?"

Hannah shook her head but was visibly disturbed.

"Are the children all right?"

She nodded.

"Then don't say another word," he insisted, urging the horse into a fast trot. "I don't want anything to intrude on the rest of our evening. We've got to have time alone, Hannah, if we're going to keep our love intact. The children mustn't constantly come first. We have to face this unitedly, and if we are to do that then we've got to nurture our marriage before the responsibility snuffs it out. We can't let it happen."

She had heard him express these ideas many times over the last few weeks, as though it was something he felt his life depended on. She knew he was probably right, but that wasn't the problem.

"Nathan, it isn't the babies," she said quietly. "It's Janette."

He knit his brows and continued on for a while in silence. "Is it anything that our going out tonight is likely to change?" he asked at last.

"I don't think so, but we need to talk to her."

"Can we talk to her when we get home?"

"I'm sure she won't go anywhere tonight, but Nathan . . ."

"Let's talk about it later tonight then."

"Oh, Nathan, she's going to run off and marry Gabriel without even telling her parents; I doubt she'll tell us or Mother either."

"Gabriel?" he asked, pulling the horse to an abrupt stop. "Are you sure, Hannah? How can you know?"

"I heard them talking when I went in."

"Maybe they were just joking."

"No, Susie was crying and asking her not to do it. Uncle Adam would be utterly devastated, Nathan, and we're responsible for her, at least in part. She came here only to help us."

"Well, should we turn back and notify Mother, or continue on to Amber Glen?"

Hannah looked at him in astonishment. He couldn't possibly be that set on their plans for the evening, not when Janette's future was so at stake.

"Did she say when they were planning to do it?" he continued.

Hannah thought a moment and tried to remember any details she had missed. "I don't remember . . . no, that's right. She said as soon as school was out."

"That's less than two weeks!" he exclaimed in shock. "I guess it makes sense; once school was out Uncle Adam wanted her home." Nathan urged the horse on faster. "We can talk to Mother tonight; right now, I think we need to get to Amber Glen."

She looked at him again in disbelief as he, glancing over to see her expression, looked confused as well.

"We've got to get a wire to Uncle Adam, Hannah, and that's the closest open station. If they can get the message to him tonight, he'll be able to catch a morning train and be here in four or five days; if we can just keep Janette away from Gabriel until then. She's only seventeen. We'll have to figure out something."

❧

The telegram was sent, after which they immediately left to notify Sarah. It was barely light as they pulled into the lane beside the white frame house. Minutes later, she had been informed and the three adults sat around the kitchen table for some time trying to decide what to do.

"We've got to talk to her," Sarah said at last.

"I sent for Uncle Adam," Nathan began, but Sarah shook her head.

"Maybe one of us should put her on the train tomorrow and take her back." She shook her head again and then rested it in her hands. "Oh Andrew," she whispered, "why did you leave me when I need you so badly?"

Nathan put his arm around his mother and held her as she struggled through her worry and resurfacing loss. She was looking old and gray, filled with fear and the dread of a promise she felt she had not been able to keep. She'd given her word to look after someone else's child, after little Janette, and yet now knew that she was slipping away without anything Sarah could do to hold her back. At last, they decided to go back together and try to talk to Janette, hoping that between them they could come up with something to say that might change her mind.

Walking into the house, they found the babies asleep and Susannah alone in the front room, huddled in a chair and crying.

"What's wrong, Susie? Where's Janette?"

"Oh, Auntie Hannah, she's outside, with Gabriel Taylor."

Nathan left the house instantly, though he could see them nowhere. By now, it was dark and his eyes were slow at adjusting from the light in the house, until he noticed a light from the barn. Making his way through the darkness he appeared at the door and saw them there in each other's arms, consumed in the passion of their kiss.

"Janette!" he declared, quite in shock.

Upon hearing his words, Gabriel instantly released the embrace and after a few more seconds he ran out the door, leaving Janette to face Nathan alone. They stood for several minutes, Nathan at a complete loss for words, and Janette's surprise gradually giving way to anger.

"You chased him off, Nathan!" she yelled at last.

"Oh, Janette, we need to talk about this."

Coming into the house and seeing Aunt Sarah as well, she gave Susannah a contemptuous look before sitting defiantly in the farthest chair she could claim from the rest of the group.

"Some friend, Susie," she muttered in angry tones, though Sarah cut her off.

"You needn't be angry at Susannah, Janette; she hasn't betrayed you at all."

Janette looked confused before resigning herself to the situation.

"Janette," Nathan began, "your parents love you very much and we love you too. They've trusted us," he shuddered, "to look after you."

"I can look after myself, Nathan; I'm not a baby you know. I'm seventeen years old. You needn't worry your head over it."

"Janette, after what I saw just now in the barn, I have to worry myself over it."

"Gabriel loves me," she began, "and I love him too."

Nathan shook his head. "No, Janette, I don't believe he does. Gabriel has done this with many young ladies. Do you think you are the first? You are simply caught up in the emotions of your passion."

"How would you know anything about what we feel for each other? You've never even talked to him about it. He's a good person, Nathan; he goes to church."

"Janette, how can you say that? Are you even aware of the things he's done in the past? Do you think that merely walking through the doors of a church for a few short months is going to entirely change him? What do you know about his character?"

"So he's made some mistakes. Why are you so against him? Don't you think he is entitled to happiness as much as yourself?"

Sitting back, Nathan realized he was getting angry and tried to calm himself down. They were both nearly yelling at each other and the room was filled with tension from it.

"Janette," he said at last, "you know that your parents would never approve."

"And why wouldn't they?" she shot back angrily.

"Because Gabriel will never make you happy in the end."

"How would you know? He has already made me happier than I've ever felt in my life and he has loved me in a way that I've never been loved before. You are the only person who is making me unhappy."

"Janette," Hannah broke in, "can you control your passions with him?" Janette looked at her blankly. "Can I explain to you how marriage works?"

"I know how it works, Hannah! Do you think I am stupid?"

"Hannah is only trying to help you," Sarah interjected. "You needn't be so hostile toward her."

Janette rolled her eyes. "All right, Hannah. How does marriage work?"

Hannah tried to ignore the sarcasm and continued as calmly as she could. "Nathan and I were friends for many years before he ever even kissed me and during that time I got to know him really well. I learned that he respected and honored me. Passion aside, by the time we decided to marry, I knew beyond doubt that he was an honest and dependable man who I could trust completely. Now that we are married and have those little babies, we are so overwhelmed by the responsibility of it that, at times, we wonder where our love has gone."

"Make your point, Hannah," she broke in impatiently.

"My point is, Janette, what if another woman came along who was attracted to Nathan and he was attracted to her? What would happen if he were the type of man who couldn't resist his passions? Where would it leave our marriage and our family? My point is that Nathan has developed an honorable character for himself and I can trust him at all times, not just those times when things are going well. Gabriel hasn't done that; he has proven his unchaste intentions far beyond doubt with several girls and he isn't treating you with respect at all. What would happen if someone was to come along that he was attracted to, and she to him? Oh, Janette, are you grown up enough to see that we only want what is good for you?"

"So, what do you want me to do, leave him completely?"

"If you could just go home and think it over for a few months, talk to your parents about it. Give yourself a chance to grow up a little more. You are still so young yet, and there is so much to learn before you get married and settle down."

Janette shot a glance at Susannah and then back to Hannah. "Who said we're getting married?"

Hannah looked down, not knowing quite what to say; if Janette knew that she had heard the earlier conversation, she might likely panic. Uncle Adam would be there in four or five days. If they could somehow keep things calm until then.

"I only hope you're not. Would you promise me that you won't?"

Janette merely stood and walked out the front door, with Sarah Layne rushing out behind her.

"Come on, Susie," Nathan said quietly. "Let me walk you home."

"Auntie Hannah?" she began. "Janette is going. . ."

"Susie, no. I heard it all while Janette was telling you. I forgot my purse and had come back in to get it. You needn't betray your friendship unnecessarily. Let's just keep it to ourselves."

Susannah nodded her understanding and then turned quietly to go.

Adam Layne arrived in the afternoon of the fifth day from the wire, coming to collect his daughter and take her home, though Janette could not be found. They searched everywhere, but it wasn't until they asked Susannah that they found she had never shown up at school that day. Instead, she had gone off toward town, refusing to speak to anyone.

Finally, in the evening she returned to Aunt Sarah's intending to collect her things. Instead, she faced a group of people sick with worry over her. Her father stood immediately.

"Janette, pack your things. We'll be leaving for home at once."

"I thought they'd wire you," she said, "but I won't be going with you."

"You'll come with me if I have to tie you up and carry you!"

"No, Papa, you won't. I am married now and I can take care of myself."

With this she turned and walked away, leaving behind a room full of shocked and heartsick people.

"You can have the marriage annulled, Adam," Sarah declared. "She's only seventeen."

Adam slumped into a chair, burying his head in his hands. "No," he said, his own voice trembling with emotion. "Sometimes, there is little more to do than to let go and let them live with the consequences of their choices."

Turning to look out the door Janette had exited only moments before, he shook his head. "It is between her and God now," he offered quietly, "and her husband."

Chapter Twenty-Three

THE FINAL WHISTLE
JUNE 1908

The day was so hot that even in the shade of the trees, the stone house beyond the brook was feeling the heat. Hannah stood guard on the babies in the front room and fanned herself to stay cool.

"Oh, Alannah, I almost forgot, you have a letter in the kitchen. Nathan brought it home the other day. It must have gotten mixed in with our mail somehow. I think the postmark said Albany."

Alannah, who was getting water ready for the wash, stopped cold.

"Where is it?" she asked carefully.

"On the counter, by the door, I think."

Turning to find the letter, she checked the postmark and went pale. With trembling hands she tried to open it, but she was shaking miserably. She felt ill and faint as she sunk into a chair at the kitchen table.

"Who's it from?" Hannah eventually called from the front room. She waited several minutes for a response and when there was no answer she called again. Finally, concerned, she got up to check, but Alannah was gone.

As she came through the front door, Mrs. Layne turned from the sink in surprise. "Why, Alannah, I thought you were over with Hannah. What's the matter dear? You are white as a sheet."

Alannah stood, trying to collect her thoughts. "Mrs. Layne, can you help Hannah today? I need to go to town."

Sarah wasn't at all sure of what was happening, but dried her hands and left quickly.

Going to Peter's room, Alannah looked around and then sat on the bed, burying her face in her hands.

"Oh, Peter," she cried to herself. "More than just my destiny, I am taking my life into my hands and your heart along with it."

Slowly, she reached for his pillow and buried her face into it. For the first time since coming to Silver Falls, Alannah freely wept bitter tears. "Oh, Peter," she cried aloud, "I may never see you again."

At last, she removed the necklace and the ring and placed them on the bed, covering them with the soft, down-filled pillow. Trying to fight back her emotion, she whispered.

"Please, forgive me."

Hearing the clock chime, Alannah hurried to her room and packed the few things together that she had brought with her all those many months ago. She scribbled a quick note and then hurried on her way. The train would be leaving in an hour. It was nearly four miles to town and she would still need to go to the bank.

Mark noticed her coming quickly into the bank with her bag and watched as she made her transaction. He heard the clerk notify her of her closed account and then watched her as she tucked the money into her purse and abruptly left.

"What the devil is going on?" he whispered to himself.

Following her outside, he could see that she was headed for the train, which was already sounding its whistle to leave. Quickly, he ran to Peter's office and burst into the room.

His brother was in process of examining an elderly man, but at Mark's appearance he excused himself and closed the door behind him.

"What's wrong?" he asked Mark.

"Alannah just closed her account at the bank and left for the train," he managed breathlessly.

"What?" Peter nearly shouted. "Mark, stay with Mr. Johnston; I'll be back as soon as I can."

The whistle sounded a final time as the young doctor headed out the door and ran with his might toward the station, though it was too late. He watched the train pull out and his heart wrenched as he saw Alannah in the window, turning away from him and covering her face with her hands. Peter stood in shock as the train disappeared down the track and around the bend. Then, slowly, he walked back to his office. If he hadn't seen it with his own eyes, he would never have believed it could be true.

Relieving Mark, he waved off his questions, asking him to leave so that he could finish his work. Mr. Johnston, who had known Peter since he was a boy, only observed quietly, trying to guess at what could reduce the young doctor from such high spirits to ashes in only minutes. Though Peter never offered a word, Mr. Johnston, being wise with a multitude of years, could sense what it must be and, feeling the burden of Peter's heart, patted him gently on the back.

"I hope it works out for you young man," he offered.

Peter looked back at him, seeing the compassion of age and experience, a certain knowing factor. He finished the examination quickly and in silence, not trusting his emotions to conversation. Then, seeing his patient out the door and having no further appointments for the day, he locked up and went home.

There were no clues to be found in her room. It looked as if it could receive her at any moment. Her dresses still filled the armoire and the medical journal she had been studying was next to the bed with the bookmark, just as she had left it the night before. Alannah thirsted after knowledge and loved reading whatever she could to learn. The journals had made for many long and interesting conversations between them in the past, blending life and death, their work and knowledge, closely together.

Peter stared at the book, deep in his own thoughts. It seemed impossible that she could leave like that. There had to be more to it. Finally, he went into his own room to rest and try to make some sense of the whole mess. It was then he discovered the note written in obvious haste.

Dear Peter,

I must go. I'm sorry. I'll love you always.

Alannah

He turned it over, hoping it might explain more on the back, but there was nothing, not even a hint as to where she'd gone, or why, or when she would be back, or if she would be back at all. Resting his head on his pillow, he noticed the dampness from her tears, then sitting and picking it up to examine it further, he saw them lying there underneath, the tokens of his love for her. She had left them behind.

"Oh, Alannah; no!" he cried out. "You mustn't be leaving for good."

Finally, he heard the door open and Hannah call out his name. He didn't want to see her; he didn't want to see anyone. The only thing Peter wanted was to be left alone.

"Peter?" she called again, at last arriving at his bedroom door. "I saw you come, but. . ."

After a glance at him, she crossed the room and sat on the bed, putting her hand on his back and rubbing it gently. Peter merely handed her the note, still reeling from the shock.

"I don't know what has happened," she said at last. "She received a letter from Albany and left immediately. Mother said she was pale when she came home and only said that she had to go to town."

"She's gone," he said in hollow tones. "Mark heard her close her account at the bank and came to tell me. I ran to the station; she was on the train, Hannah; I saw her."

To himself, he was thinking that it had to be Maggie, but why would she leave without him? And why, why leave the tokens of their love behind, the certain message that said she did not expect to return?

Peter could only wonder and ache.

Chapter Twenty-Four

The Plot
July 1908

Nathan stood on the porch, breathing deeply. He could almost smell it. Why was that? Surveying the crops all around him, he could also see it. They were ready for the harvest!

John had planted the acreage surrounding their mother's home, and Nathan knew in a few days they would need to begin the work of bringing it all in. The process would go on for weeks, and with Peter so busy in town, it meant that he and John alone would be responsible for the other acres as well.

Hannah walked out to join him, putting her arm through his and resting her head against his shoulder.

"Are they down for naps?" he asked.

"Yes, finally. We have two hours, more or less."

"What needs to be done?" Nathan ventured.

"Oh, everything, I guess," she sighed.

It was the usual routine of late, trying to get ready for the harvest, when he would have to be unavailable for anything else. All of the chores and projects that had been put off over the last ten months, as well as anything at all that would need to be done over the next two or three in the future, would need to happen now.

"What do you want me to do first?"

Hannah snuggled into his shoulder. "None of it, Nathan; absolutely none of it."

Nathan laughed as they sat down on the porch. "I know the feeling. What would you like to do if you had a couple of hours to yourself then?"

"Oh, you know, go down to the beach with my husband and walk in the sand, maybe get our toes a little wet, hold hands."

Looking back at the house holding their three sleeping children, he smiled. "Well, that's out. Anything else?"

She snuggled into him a little more. "Do you know what I really want? I want to sit here in the quiet, with your arms around me, listening to the wind in the trees and feeling the breeze on my face, and I want you to love me, Nathan. I just want to be held and loved in the quiet."

Nathan raised his eyebrows and smiled. "There's always the swing."

Hannah agreed and, after a short walk across the yard and getting settled, they began to sway in long, slow passes, out over by the brook and back several times.

"Oh, Nathan," she sighed, leaning back against him. "When was it last that we took the time to do this?"

He smiled and shook his head. "Too long ago, Hannah love, and I'm afraid it will be a while before we'll be able to do it again. If this weather keeps up, the harvest will be ready before the end of the week."

"Oh," she said despondently, "the harvest. Why do we have to plant so much? We can't even begin to use it all and we don't need the money from selling so much of it. I envy Davy over there," she said, gesturing across the fields. "He doesn't own half as many acres and he never plants the entire thing; yet they have plenty for their family."

He nodded as he put his arm around her. "You know, Hannah, we talk about the idea of horses every year about this time. Why is it that we never follow through with it?"

"I don't know, but every year as I look out at the enormity of the chore and think of you working so hard in the heat, collapsing so exhausted into bed each night, and hardly having a chance to speak to you or be with you, it's then that I always wish we had."

"I suppose I could turn it all into pasture and work at the bank. Mark has been pressuring me to put in more hours there."

"Then you wouldn't have time for the horses."

"True."

"Besides, I would be terribly lonely if I couldn't look out and see you during the day."

Nathan smiled. "Then let's do it this year, after the harvest. In the meantime, do you have any last requests before it begins?"

"Only the fence."

He looked around the yard. "Tell me again where you want it to go."

"Just around the yard, pretty much where the grass is. It needs to be big enough for the babies to play, but small enough to keep them out of the brook."

"You'll have no help this summer, will you?"

"Your mother said she'd still come if I need her."

"Has anyone heard from Alannah yet?" he asked.

"No, not yet."

"That's too bad. Peter seems to feel certain he'll hear from her eventually. Why do you suppose she left?"

"No one knows. The note only said that she had to leave, that she was sorry, and good-bye. It's amazing that Peter could find no trace of her when he went to Albany. It's as though she has disappeared from the face of the earth."

Nathan shook his head. "I liked Alannah. I can't imagine why she would do that."

"Yes, but I suppose it at least opened up a job for Janette. If there was any good to come of it, then I guess it was that; though it hardly seems fitting to call it so." Hannah shook her head. "Poor Janette, she's been working so hard while Gabriel merely sits around his parents' house, and she being so sick with the baby. She is determined to make it work though."

"She does have a will about her, doesn't she?" Nathan mused. "It's as if she feels she must prove everyone wrong, no matter what the personal sacrifice to herself. I'm afraid she's chosen a hard life. Maybe I should offer Gabriel a job helping with the harvest."

"I mentioned that possibility already, but she said he doesn't like getting all that dirt under his fingernails."

Nathan laughed out loud. "Well, there are gloves to use, and there's nothing that says you can't wash your hands at the end of the day. Is there anything he does like to do?"

"I asked the same question. Janette said he would like to be a professional 'taster' in a restaurant."

Nathan laughed heartily again. "Not much chance of that around here."

"No; but you know that Janette defends him through and through, and she said he is a good cook."

"So, she works all day while he stays at home and cooks?"

"Yes, something like that."

They were silent for a while as the swing continued making quiet passes across the yard. Finally, Nathan spoke.

"Hannah, do you suppose he might be interested in opening a restaurant in town?"

"I don't know that Silver Falls would have enough business to support one."

"No, but what if they built one close to the train station. If it was a nice place, with a classy reputation like The Springs, people would come from all around to go to it; wouldn't you think?"

"Possibly," Hannah agreed. "The Springs did have quite a reputation."

"And think of the jobs it would provide for the community." Nathan kissed his wife. "Hannah, could you imagine how wonderful it would be to have a restaurant like that in town?"

"Yes, nearly as wonderful as another kiss like that."

He smiled and kissed her again. "Why don't you invite them over for dinner, before the harvest begins, and I'll try to figure out a way to approach it with them."

"You'll have to make it sound easy."

❧

The meal was arranged, and Susannah agreed to tend the babies at her own house, so as to provide the ideal environment for the "proposal" to be presented. Toward the end of dinner, as they all sat around the table finishing the last of the meal, Janette mentioned how delicious it was.

This was Hannah's cue to say her part. They were hoping that at least one of them would offer a compliment, but if not then Nathan would. Regardless, Hannah had her cue and their script was ready to unfold.

"Thank you," she answered. "It isn't quite like eating at The Springs, but it keeps us nourished and healthy."

"Ah, The Springs!" Nathan exclaimed with feeling. "Hannah, love, do you remember what a night at The Springs was like?"

Hannah tried to remain serious, but being an actress with memorized lines was not at all her forte. Nathan really had much more the flair for it. However, it was a worthy cause and she had agreed to do her best.

"It was heavenly, wasn't it?" she returned, as wistfully as possible.

"Yes, heavenly is a good word; truly a rich man's paradise."

The words "rich man" had caught Gabriel's ear, as Nathan had hoped they would, and he waited a slight moment for him to respond.

"Was it an expensive place?" he asked.

Nathan mulled over the question, casting a glance at Hannah, who tried hard not to smile, and then another over to Janette.

"No, I wouldn't say it was too terribly expensive. I think I was referring more to the owner of it. I heard he was a very wealthy man, though the restaurant does look a little like paradise; do you remember, love?"

"Yes, with the ferns and trellises."

"And those fancy waiters."

"And the band," Janette added.

"Why, Janette," Nathan teased, "how did you know that The Springs had a band?"

"I have been there, Nathan," she insisted, a certain tone of indignation to her voice.

"And did the waiters know your name?" he teased further.

"Well, they knew Papa's name. Everyone knew my father's name," she added in a little tone of melancholy.

Nathan had to smile to himself; Janette had fallen for it. "Yes, I always felt a little like a king to be greeted by one of those fancy waiters. 'Ah hello, Mr. Layne,' they would say. 'So nice to see you again; may I get a table for you and your wife?' "

This was Hannah's cue again. "Yes; and then do you remember how we would dance into the night? It was so romantic."

Janette had mentioned that Gabriel especially loved dancing.

"Could you imagine what a king you would feel," Nathan continued, "to own such an establishment as that? You could walk in with your top hat and gold tipped cane and they would greet you with 'Good evening, Mr. Layne,' or, 'Good evening, Mr. Taylor. May I get the best table for you and your wife?' "

Hannah held her breath at the transition, but Gabriel was getting quite involved in the entire fantasy.

"Yes, it's too bad there's nothing like that around here," Nathan declared. "But goodness, what I'd do if I owned a restaurant like that. Why, I might even build myself a large house in town."

"And buy a motor car," Hannah added.

"I'd have electricity," Janette ventured.

"What about you, Gabriel," Nathan broke in. "What would you do?"

"I'd have maids and butlers to do all of my bidding," he said importantly.

"Wouldn't that be nice, Hannah, to know an important person with maids and butlers? Yes, when people referred to 'Mr. Taylor', we could say 'We know him; he married our cousin.' Well, it's too bad there isn't anything like that around here; and with that spot by the train station so perfect and available. People could come from miles around to eat there. What an addition to the community it would be. You know, I bet the bank would even be willing to back a venture like that to get it started. What do you think, Hannah?"

"Maybe so, honey."

It was obvious, even to Hannah, that Gabriel had taken the bait completely. Nathan winked at his wife across the table with a satisfied look on his face.

"Well," he said at last. "I guess it's time to get the children before they fall asleep in the wrong house."

Janette and Gabriel stood to leave with obvious gleam in their eyes.

"All in a good day's work," Nathan whispered to Hannah as they left. "I'd give them no more than a week before we see Janette in the bank."

Hannah laughed. " 'The Falls,' that's what I'd call it."

Chapter Twenty-Five

Mansions Ahead
August 1908

"Hannah, do you think Nathan was serious about the restaurant and the bank?"

Exactly four days had elapsed since the night of the dinner, and Janette had quietly pulled Hannah aside after church to pursue the matter further. Taking a thoughtful glance in the other direction, she tried to compose the ideas Nathan had shared with her into words.

"Why do you ask? Is Gabriel interested in the idea?"

"Interested?" Janette laughed. "Why, he has drawn up the entire menu, compiled a list of possible employees and wants to make a trip to Colorado to check out firsthand how The Springs is run. I've never seen him so excited about anything. It's all he has talked about for the last four days."

Hannah tried valiantly to contain her joy, but it was almost too good to be true. Her smiles of delight at Janette's obvious hopefulness could not be contained.

"Is he planning to be the professional taster of the establishment?" she teased.

"Sort of; maybe head chef would be a closer title."

"I'll ask him, Janette," she winked. "I'm sure he wasn't teasing completely, but the harvest is on us and I don't know that he'll have enough extra time to bring it up at the bank right now. Since his dad died, the workload is too much for him and John alone. If he only had a little more help, but I guess men are busy around these parts this time of year. I'll talk to him about it tonight and let you know."

Janette's face was all hopefulness as they parted, she to her lone buggy, and Hannah to find Nathan and share the good news.

A look of satisfaction stole its way across his face as the conversation between them unfolded.

"This is splendid, love. I had no idea he'd be quite that receptive to it. This is all just splendid. We'll have to figure out a way to fund it under cover of the bank. If you see Janette before I do, have her send Gabriel out to talk to me."

Neither of them had the time to worry about it further, between the rush of collecting the babies after church and getting everyone home, fed, bathed, and to bed. They had barely sat down in the front room to enjoy a moment of peace when they heard a buggy in the lane. Looking out, they saw the Taylors pass by one of the windows.

Quickly, leaving their places of repose and gathering the armloads of triplet debris, they rushed to stash it into an inconspicuous corner. Then, in the next minute, they were welcoming their cousins in.

"Gabriel, Janette," Nathan began; "do come in. What brings you out here this evening?"

Gabriel tossed an apprehensive glance at Janette as he whispered. "I thought you talked to them already."

"We were wondering if we could talk to you about the restaurant idea." she announced.

Nathan tossed a wink at his wife as he welcomed them in. "What did you have in mind?" he began, not being sure which of the two to address.

"Go ahead, Gabriel. It was your idea; ask him," Janette urged.

They sat in quiet anticipation for more than a moment before he finally swallowed hard and began to speak.

"Well, Nathan, we've been thinking about that restaurant idea you mentioned the other night. I did some asking around and found some cousins and one of my brothers who'd be interested in building it, if I could somehow come up with enough money for funding. We were wondering about the bank? We don't have much for collateral besides a very little bit of savings, but I understand that you might be able to use some hired help with your harvest this summer. We also thought we might visit Janette's father as well and, you know, see what we could work out there."

Nathan sat back in his chair and stroked his chin thoughtfully, exerting all of his energies to try and remain serious. "This is a big undertaking, Gabe. Are you sure you've thought it through?"

"I've hardly thought of anything else. Several members of the family want to work in it once it's going and I've figured most of the operating down to the finest detail. Friday, I went out to Amber Glen and talked with Mr. Christians about what it took to run his place. We figure Janette could do the bookwork at home once the baby is here. Mother and I can do the cooking and my cousin James and a few others have agreed to be waiters. Everyone has agreed to work on a profit-sharing basis until we can get it all established." He paused before continuing. "There's just the slight problem of funds to get it all built and going. We were wondering what it would take to get a loan with the bank and what would be required with payments and, well, you know, all the details of something like that."

Sitting back in his chair, Nathan let the silence hang suspensefully in the room. "I could use some help in the fields, to be sure, and I'd be willing to pay you well for it. If any of your family can work I'd be willing to pay them also. They could go in with you as part owners. I'd suspect Uncle Adam would be interested in a venture proposition such as this. Besides, he knows the owner of The Springs personally. I'll bet he could arrange an interview with him to discuss the details of running such a high-class establishment. Yes," he said, stroking his chin once again, as if deep in thought, "I think Uncle Adam would be most pleased about an arrangement like this. Have you made plans to visit him right away?"

"We were thinking towards the end of the month, but we could make it a little later if necessary, considering the harvest. I could start working on that tomorrow, if you like."

"Yes, I'd like that very much. I'll pay you on a per-acre basis. If you want to use your crop earnings as earnest money, I'll even present the business end of the proposition to Janette's father."

Gabriel stood in jubilant relief. "Well then, if it's to be per acre, I suppose I shall get myself home and to bed as soon as possible so as to be here bright and early. Thank you, Nathan," he added, as sincerely as he could, shaking his hand with gusto.

As the door closed behind their guests, Nathan smiled and sat back down triumphantly.

"This is going well, Hannah; wouldn't you say? He certainly took the bait, and it will be interesting to see how willing he is to get a little grit under those fingernails of his after all."

"Do you think you'll write to Uncle Adam soon?"

"Write? Absolutely not. I'll send a wire to him tomorrow as soon as I can get Gabriel going in the fields. I want to offer a personal guarantee on the entire venture before they ever talk to him."

Hannah smiled to herself. Nathan's heart was a good one, and she hoped his intentions for this cousin and her spouse worked out to the fullest measure.

Gabriel showed up as bright and early as he had promised, along with a crew of cousins to aid in the work. Since it was to be payment per acre, he wanted to take as full of an advantage as possible in securing their hopeful future professions and wealth.

What would normally have lasted many weeks for Nathan and John was completed by the Taylor clan in less than two, and it was well that it did, for the weather was warmer than usual and the grain crop ripened all at once.

Adam Layne was very receptive to the restaurant idea, owing to a hope for his daughter's welfare and future, not to mention Nathan's careful planning, assurance, and guarantee of financial solvency. Before summer's end, the whole operation was rolling along through construction.

The Taylors showed themselves to be masterful in their efforts at advertising, proving the old adage that when there is a will, there is a way. Due to their enticing allurements, most of the town and many of the surrounding communities were waiting with great anticipation of having such a fine establishment to grace their humble area.

As for Gabriel, he worked with a heretofore unknown determination each day, collapsing in his bed when night came, exhausted, but with the vision of millions, mansions, and servants in his dreams. The building was nearing completion by late fall, holding within it Gabriel's ambitions to further the refinement of the area, taking it and himself to a quality of "greatness," never to return!

Chapter Twenty-Six

Love Letters
November 1908

The last few rays of autumn sunshine began to dim over the horizon as Nathan secured everything to its place in the barn for the night. Taking a last look around to see that nothing had been missed, he watered the several horses and tossed a little more hay into their stalls. Finally, he paused at the door of the barn to assess one last time how everything was being kept under the new arrangements. Having acquired several fine brood mares at the end of harvest, he had spent the last of summer and most of the early fall building fences and planting pasture.

The rains had been slower than usual in coming this year, but the grass was at last beginning to grow, and he hoped the pasture would be sufficiently ready for the herd by spring. For now, the horses, which had only one large paddock and a portion of the barn to share for shelter, would just have to be content with their makeshift and somewhat cramped quarters.

Closing up for the night, he turned his attentions to the house. Through the windows, he could see Hannah trying to get dinner on the table, and even from the barn he could hear the dull roar of mayhem making its way outside.

Poor Hannah, she looked tired and harried. The babies had been sick a few days earlier and had tested her patience to its limit with their crankiness. With his work on the pasture and fences demanding so much time, Nathan knew he had been precious little help to her. It had been a long week for them both, but catching a glimpse of her face as he came through the kitchen door, he guessed it had been longest for her.

"Hi, love," he whispered, kissing her on the cheek. "What's next?"

"If you can corral the babies into their highchairs as well as you do those horses," she began, "then I think we should be about ready to eat."

He had to smile at the phrasing of the request. Perhaps "roping and hog tying" would be a more accurate term. Either way, he began the task quickly.

"Your mother should be here in about ten minutes, Nathan, and we haven't even started dinner or their baths."

"My mother? Isn't Susie coming tonight?"

"No, she had something else come up; but your mother has generously volunteered to take the children for the night, if we can get them fed and ready for bed here in the very near future."

After capturing Melanie and strapping her into her seat, he paused for a moment, smiling to himself. Andrew was already in place and Meredith, seeing an open opportunity for more play, had escaped into the other room, running and squealing with delight in grand anticipation of a chase from daddy.

"Will she be watching them here then, or at her house?"

"I don't suppose it would be much of a break to have them sleep over with your mother here. No, they're spending the night over there and the idea of it is the only thing that has gotten me through the last of this day."

With the final baby retrieved and put in place, they sat down and began dishing up the children's plates. Almost immediately after, a knock sounded at the front door.

"Oh, it's your mother and we haven't even begun."

"Relax, Hannah; she won't mind. I'll let her in."

Sarah emerged seconds later, joining them all at the table where the children were busily throwing food at each other and onto the floor, occasionally getting a morsel or so past the ears and nose and into the proper cavity.

"You look exhausted, Hannah; are you all right?"

"Yes, Mother, I'm fine; it's just been a long week. I'm sorry we're running so behind. Have you eaten?"

"Yes. Are their things packed?"

"No, I haven't gotten that far."

"Then eat up. I'll take care of it and I can bathe them all at my house. You look as if you could use the break. Son, when you're finished, why don't you help get everyone home with me and we'll give your good wife a moment off."

She was off to pack a bag and within twenty minutes the little Laynes were being carried out the front door and off to Grandma's.

Hannah leaned forward, intending to rest her head on the table, but after noticing all the food debris, she reconsidered and instead slumped further into her chair. The house was quiet at last, and still, even more still than in the middle of the night. She would savor that rare silence while it lasted.

What ecstasy to have a moment alone! She breathed deeply and then listened. How long had it been since she had heard the clock ticking or noticed the stove crackling as it does? Sitting back up, she finished the last of her dinner and then slowly pushed her chair from the table and began cleaning up the baby mess.

Even when she had finished, Nathan had still not returned, so she hung her apron on the hook near the pantry and made her way to the sofa in the front room. There, she settled down to watch the flames in the fireplace dance in their hypnotic way. Nearby was a box which, when she spied it, made her heart jump to realize that it had been left within the babies' realm of destruction. However, she calmed once she discovered that it had somehow, miraculously, been spared.

It was the box containing Nathan's love letters, which he had written from his trips to Colorado. These were the letters he had written and never sent, never intending her to read, and which contained words of entertainment that could bring delight to even her dreariest of days. Retrieving it, she carefully opened the top, thumbing through to find her favorites. Ah yes, this one was a definite. Lying back down on the couch, she began slowly re-reading it, savoring each word.

January 3rd, 1901

My dearest, loveliest Hannah,

I've recently returned from a walk through town, by myself. It has been snowing for days, but the moon is out tonight casting its glow all over the world, and how I longed for you to be here. I longed to walk with you, just the two of us, across the frozen fields and I ached to hold you in my arms and tell you . . .

Her thoughts were interrupted by her husband coming in the front door, shedding his coat and boots by the entry and giving his wet hair a shake.

"It's raining again. Mother said not to worry about the babies, we can pick them up tomorrow whenever we like. I was thinking that if the weather lets up we could take one of those rides down to the beach in the morning." He then paused as he surveyed the situation.

"Nathan, can you come read this to me?"

"Oh no, not the letters," he laughed with a certain mock teasing to his voice.

"Please, honey. Just let me lie here with my head in your lap and play with my hair the way you used to, and read your letters to me. Read them the way you wrote them, with all the same feeling. Please?"

Nathan merely smiled and shook his head. "All right, Hannah. Sit up a moment so I can get settled. Where did you leave off?"

"Start right here."

Glancing over the contents he smiled. "Yes, this one has promise, doesn't it? I must say I'm relieved you didn't choose the most embarrassing one this time. Let's see now."

I ached to hold you in my arms and tell you all of the feelings of my heart. Oh, Hannah, my love, if you could only be here with me now, in the moonlight and freshly fallen snow, alone in the night. Would you like to know what I would do?

"Oh, yes!" she interrupted.

First, I would take you in my arms and hold you as close as I could, and then, Hannah, I would kiss your soft crimson lips and run my fingers through your hair, drinking in all the warmth of your sweet love. And with the moon shining just so, I would ask you to marry me. I would say, 'Hannah, my love, will you be my wife, will you love me forever?' For now, I will have to imagine that you will say yes. Then after we're married, there's a certain cabin in the mountains here. A popular place in the summer, but quiet in the winter; it is utterly beautiful. I would take you there, where we could be completely alone, snowbound . . .

Nathan put the letter back in the box and stopped short.

"Oh, Nathan, don't stop now! This is the best part, please don't stop!"

Nathan kissed his wife. "You know what it says, Hannah, you've probably read it already this week anyway. Besides, it's too embarrassing to read out loud; what if someone was listening? We'll have to burn those letters before our children ever learn to read."

"Oh, no! You'll do no such thing, Nathan Layne. Those are my letters! You gave them to me, remember? They are my life and breath on days like this one has been. I would sooner die than lose them. Please, just read the rest of it. It is so romantic."

Nathan smiled, standing up and pulling a very reluctant Hannah up as well, holding her close and saying, "Hannah, my love, it is raining right now and while there is no moon to speak of, our children are off at their grandmother's for the night, and we are completely alone. Why read of this sort of thing when I can kiss your soft crimson lips here and now and hold you close to me and drink in your love?" He smiled and held her close as he kissed her tenderly. "What do you say?"

Hannah laughed and sat back down, fishing the letter back from the box. "I say you should finish reading the letter to me first, and then we'll discuss any possible fantasies you may have harbored at the time. You know, it was really quite romantic of you. I never knew you had it in you back then."

"I assure you I did!" he laughed. "Though, at times, it is embarrassing to admit I ever put half of those ideas into writing. Most of them are innocent enough, I suppose. I used to read them to myself and fantasize of sending them to you. Sounds a little strange now, but it was sort of comforting at the time. I can tell I should have never included this one in the box; I had no idea you'd read it the way you do. Goodness, Hannah, if someone else ever got hold of it,

I would die from the embarrassment. What if Reverend Sanderson ever saw it? I think we should burn them right now."

"Not in a million years," she insisted, holding it out of his reach. "No one will ever read them but me. I promise."

"And how can you be so sure? Oh, very well," he said reluctantly. "Hand it over."

"Promise you won't burn it?"

"Yes," he laughed, "I promise. Now, where was I?"

"Half way down the first page, where it says alone in the mountains, in the snow-bound cabin."

"Oh, here we are."

. . . where we could be completely alone, snowbound, just the two of us . . .

They were interrupted by a knock at the door, which Nathan, thankfully, got up to answer, leaving Hannah to bury her frustration in her hands.

"Peter, hello; come in. What are you doing out in the rain?"

"Peter, what timing," she whispered under her breath.

"I thought I'd stop by and say hi before going home," he answered in a voice full of blue. "Are the babies asleep already? I was rather hoping they would still be up."

"Actually, Mother has them," Nathan answered.

"Yes, she's keeping them for the entire night," Hannah added, hopeful that he might pick up on the hint.

He didn't.

Instead he settled himself into the chair nearest the fire and stared at the flames for a long while, completely oblivious of any intrusion. Hannah discreetly put the letter back into the box and casually pushed it all under the couch with her foot.

"What's the matter, Peter?" she asked, at last summoning enough compassion to take notice of his dampened clothes and dampened spirits alike.

Peter looked off into the fire. "Oh, I don't know. Life seems like it should have more to it sometimes. Like your life, Nathan, and John's, with a wife and children. Sometimes it just feels so purposeless anymore."

"Any word from Alannah?" Nathan asked.

Looking quite disheartened, Peter answered that there hadn't been so much as a hint about her.

"Maybe you should look around. Surely there are other available women in the area. There must be someone who could help fill the void and offer a little romance to your life."

"Romance?" Peter questioned. "I think I've forgotten what the word means."

"Yes, I can understand that," Hannah muttered.

They sat in silence a while longer, listening to the wood crackle in the hearth, before Peter finally stood to leave.

"Well, I guess I'll leave you both to your night alone. Mother will be wondering where I am. Besides, it sounds as if the more active part of the family is over there anyway. I really did want to see the babies tonight. You're lucky to have such a family, Nathan. I very much envy you."

They stood to see him to the door and watched a little while as he drove down the lane toward home.

"Romance?" Hannah questioned. "What makes him think we have more romance than he does?" She was smiling, though Nathan wasn't very amused with the teasing.

"It is sad, Hannah; he loved Alannah dearly. It's a great loss to him. I hope he didn't hear your comments. It was a bit rude, don't you think?"

"You could hear that? I'm sorry; it just slipped out. There really is nothing we can do to help the situation though. I suppose it is like anything else that time has to heal."

"I'm tired, love; let's go to bed."

"Oh, no; you're not getting out of it that easily."

They settled back onto the couch and Nathan retrieved the box, thumbing through the papers.

"How about this one? This is a fine love letter."

My dearest Hannah,

This is my third letter to you today and it is only noon, but my heart is aching for you. If only I could be home, or if only you could be here. How I would love to see your eyes again, looking into mine, to hear the music of your laughter and feel your gentle touch. Oh, Hannah, if I could only feel my arms around you once again, and if only we could sit before the fire and be together. I feel consumed in my loneliness for you today, and I'm afraid I've been of little use at work. Mostly I've stared out the window and wondered what you are doing right now, wishing I could be there to share in whatever it is.

"Oh, not that one, Nathan; it isn't romantic at all. It sounds entirely lonely."

Looking over the page he shrugged to himself. "I thought it was quite romantic."

She looked at him square and shook her head. "No, it isn't romantic at all."

Moving the box aside and settling her head in his lap once again, she returned the original object of debate to his hands, trying to get cozy and comfortable. Nathan gathered her hair up in a twist and caressed the side of her cheek as she snuggled more closely.

"The letter," she urged.

"Oh, Hannah, your skin is like satin; I don't need snowbound cabins to feel romantic about you."

"Maybe not; but it has been a long week and I want to hear it just the same."

There was, at that moment, another knock at the door.

"Now what?" she exclaimed.

They didn't have to wait long, for Susannah, breathless and wet, was letting herself in, shedding her jacket and wet shoes and apologizing profusely for being late.

"I'm sorry, Auntie Hannah, but Mother is in a real temper tonight. I told her I'd run an errand for her, but forgot. Then I said I'd fix dinner, but forgot that too, and then I didn't do the mending because I was distracted by something else. Finally, she said I had to clean the kitchen and help get the twins to bed before I went anywhere. I suppose I don't blame her for getting so upset, but she wouldn't even let me run over to say I'd be late. I'm really sorry."

Susannah seemed to manage the entire speech in one breath, never noticing the quiet lamplight and cozy scene before her, or the missing squeals of the babies.

"You said you had other plans for tonight, Susie. Nathan's mother has the children at her house for the evening."

"Plans?" she repeated blankly. All at once, her eyes flew wide open and her hands covered her mouth. "Oh, my gosh! I forgot!" she said, quickly grabbing her things and putting them back on. "Oh, Auntie Hannah, I'm afraid I've lost my memory completely today. There's the quilting social tonight in town and they were going to pick me up for it. What time is it? Oh, maybe if I hurry I can get back home before they get there. Bye."

She was gone before they had stirred from their places, and the Laynes were left to smile at the whirlwind of teenage life and exuberance that had spun in and spun back out of their home. Hannah looked quietly over the paper before handing it back to her husband.

"I've always heard that the third time is a charm."

He was about to say something in agreement when they both heard the carriage wheels in the lane and within moments another knock sounded at the door.

"Oh, for goodness sakes!" she exclaimed. "What now? How is it that so much of the town is out on this rainy night and finding our home as the desired place of destination? Are we not meant to be alone? Maybe someone has placed a curse on our privacy!"

Nathan only laughed and, getting up to answer the door, was met by a carriage full of young ladies.

"Mrs. Harrison said we'd find Susie here," the one young lady began.

"She's gone back home," Hannah called from the couch. "I think she temporarily forgot all about it, but you should find her at home now."

As they turned their horses around and started back down the lane, leaving the two of them quite alone at last, Nathan closed the door and this time locked it.

"It's hopeless. Who do you suppose will show up next?" Hannah asked. "The sheriff, or maybe the president?"

"I don't know; let's just blow out the light before they do and maybe they'll go away."

"It's hard to read in the dark," she reminded him, holding up the letter a last time.

"Ah, yes," he said thoughtfully, "and where were we with that, anyway?"

Hannah smiled a final, faint hopefulness to him. "Where we could be completely alone, snowbound, just the two of us."

"Hmmm," he said, walking to the mantle and blowing out the lamps, leaving only the light of the fire to cast dancing shadows across the room.

"Oh, Nathan," she moaned, genuinely disappointed.

"Hannah, my love," he said, taking her hands and pulling her up from the couch, "that part of the letter I will always have memorized." He kissed his wife. "And, in the end, it would be easier to tell you with the lights out."

Chapter Twenty-Seven

Paper Clips and Promises
December 1908

The whistle blew notice of the train's departure while, trembling, she wondered whether she should really stay or if, in futility, she should re-board and take it to a further destination. She stood in her indecision a while longer in the small station, a baby in her arms and a carpet bag filled with their meager possessions at her side.

The cold, torrential rain coursed down the windows and filled the streets as if threatening to wash half the world away with it. She hadn't so much as an umbrella to her name, most of the contents of the bag merely being necessities for her daughter.

Having spent the little bit of her remaining money for the train fare, she stood at the window, nearly penniless, staring out at the storm and reflecting on the similarly bleak conditions of her own future. She couldn't even be sure from where their next meal might come. It was craziness to spend her last few dollars for the fare, but her conscience demanded that it be used no other way. She had an apology to make and she knew she could not rest until it was done.

"A mite stormy outside, ma'am," the stationmaster said, breaking into her thoughts. "Not quite the day for a stroll with a baby. Where you headed?"

"The doctor's."

Although it was only around the corner, he offered her a ride, and soon Alannah found herself standing on the boardwalk in front of Peter's office. Trying the door, she found it unlocked and so went inside. After listening another minute, she could hear the familiar sounds of an examination going on in the next room, with Peter's cheerful voice explaining each step of the procedure to an obviously nervous patient.

Alannah smiled to herself as she recalled his "nervous patient routine." She had heard it many times and she had longingly missed the man to whom it belonged.

Sitting down at the desk, she transferred Maggie to her lap as a warm familiarity crept over her heart. She opened the book and, turning back to June, found her own neat script recording the day's keeping. The handwriting changed to Peter's own after she had left, and then to another's she didn't recognize. It wasn't neat or very organized, and leafing through the pages she quickly noticed several obvious errors. She found that same handwriting continue up through November and a few days into December. At that point, it changed back to Peter's again and continued so over two weeks of entries up to today, Thursday, December 19, 1908.

The entries were all hurried and incomplete, and her heart ached at the knowledge of the extra hardship her leaving had undoubtedly caused, not only in the ledger, but in the heart of the doctor as well. He had loved her and trusted her.

Alannah could feel herself begin to tremble again. She couldn't expect any of it to be the same. That was over six months ago. She owed them all so much, and yet she had nothing to give, nothing except an apology.

The door opened and she heard Peter's farewells as the gentleman came out, leaving the doctor to put his things away. Nodding to her, the man tipped his hat and then hurried off into the storm, down the street and around a corner.

Maggie, who had been sitting very quietly on her mother's lap up until now, reached for the feather pen and knocked over an open box of clips, sending them falling to the floor. Alannah quickly stooped down to gather them up, but not before Peter heard the noise and, thinking he may have missed a patient, came to the door. Stunned at the sight of her, he was nearly speechless.

"Alannah!" he exclaimed at last.

"Hello, Peter," she said, standing and brushing the loose hairs from her face. Both continued to face each other in silence as Peter tried to gather his wits. Finally, he came to the desk and bent down to the little girl.

"Hello, little one," he offered in friendly tones. "You must be Maggie." Picking her up, he brushed the curls from her forehead and then smiled at Alannah. "It is obvious who she belongs to, isn't it? She's as beautiful as her mother. I trust she will be my newest patient?"

"No, Peter. We haven't come to require anything more of you. I only wanted to ask your forgiveness. It wasn't right to leave the way I did, and I'm sorry. I really couldn't see any other option. I didn't know what else to do."

"I would have gone with you."

"No, it couldn't be risked. It would only have jeopardized all of our lives. I had to act quickly to get Maggie back or I would have lost the chance forever. I'm not asking anything from you, except your forgiveness. It is the only unresolved thing left in my life that matters."

Peter smiled and caressed her cheek. "My forgiveness?" he laughed softly. "It is certainly not the only unresolved thing that matters in my life. I believe we had an appointment to keep that you full well missed."

Alannah's heart nearly stopped. Quickly, she bent down again to the floor to finish picking up the clips.

"I'm sorry, Peter," she said quietly. "You can't know how I wanted to keep it. I just wasn't able." She was quiet a while more, until he knelt down to help her. "I haven't come to beg you to take me back," she added, deeply embarrassed by the entire situation, "only to ask your forgiveness. If you will grant me that, then I will leave."

"And where are you planning to go?" he asked. "It is a dickens of a night to be traveling with a baby and no umbrella."

Smiling at her, Peter took her hand and helped her to her feet. "Come home with me, Alannah. We can fix up a room for Maggie and talk about this further under more comfortable circumstances."

He knew she would try to hide it, but the lingering hope he saw in her eyes strengthened his resolves. Tenderly, he lifted her chin and kissed her, meeting no resistance.

Finally, smiling and hoisting Maggie in his arms, he tickled her briefly under the chin. "Come, little Maggie, and meet the finest grandma you'll ever know." He grabbed his coat and turned to Alannah again before opening the door.

"Alannah, my love, I have waited months for you to return, and I will grant my forgiveness freely; but leaving me again to wallow in my loneliness hardly seems a fitting repentance to my thinking. It would seem much more appropriate to me if you simply stayed. We can talk it over further after dinner, say, in front of the fire and after this little one goes to bed. For now, please, let's just go home."

Chapter Twenty-Eight

SPEAKING OUT OF TURN
JANUARY 1909

The new year arrived in style, ringing merrily in with the bells of Peter and Alannah's wedding. There was little reason for them to wait, really. It had all been planned for and arranged before she ever left. The actual honeymoon had to be put off a little while, though it was of very little consequence to Peter, who was especially happy just to have it all official and complete.

Life didn't change so very much for them at all, since Sarah had asked them to stay on with her. Maggie was happy and comfortable in her new home, while Alannah was altogether relieved with her own change of status.

"Mrs. Doctor Layne," was what the local folk were now inclined to call her, or "Mrs. Doctor," for those who felt a more familiar need to shorten it. Her worries over what people might say about the circumstance of her daughter appeared to be unfounded.

Over the years, the Laynes had grown to become pillars of the Silver Falls community and if there were ever any hints of less than positive talk, then it never went far enough to reach the ears of anyone close to the family. They were married in the church, Peter had adopted Maggie, and mother and child were both frankly accepted as local kin from that point on.

Things were going very well in the white clapboard home that Andrew Layne had built, as was life in the little stone house across the fields and over the brook. For Nathan, Hannah, and the babies, it had pretty much settled into a workable routine over the months. The children were thriving, and as winter passed and spring came wafting in, they merely continued to flourish and grow as they had been.

Meredith generally led the group in each new development. She had been the first to sit, to crawl, to walk, and to speak; she also commonly appeared to mastermind their mischief. Mellie and Andy looked to her as a sort of herald for their development. Whatever Merrie did, the others knew they should be trying it next as well.

Enchanted by her cleverness, she was also something of a diva to Alannah's daughter, who found her new cousin's skill set to be nothing short of fascinating. Due to her unfortunate start in life, Maggie had been a bit delayed in her development, though thanks to Meredith and the others, she was learning quickly now. Much to Alannah's relief, Merrie and Maggie hit it off right away.

Once the rains of spring had passed and the warmth of summer was making a regular appearance, the triplets began begging to be allowed out to the yard as often as their parents would permit.

On this particular day, the warm July sun filtered gently through the leaves of the giant maples. A soft breeze pushed the high, cumulous clouds peacefully through the sky, while closer to the earth, an occasional butterfly could be spotted carelessly fluttering here and there. The very air seemed filled with a quiet peacefulness, which in turn wrought a restful mood over the entire farm.

Several of the mares, having foaled, were lazily grazing on the sweet pasture grass as their young frolicked in the sunshine. Nathan was with them in the field, giving them grain and brushing down their sleek coats while occasionally trying to familiarize the foals to being touched and handled.

Coming to Dolly, he began the brushing process anew, speaking to her in gentle tones and eventually slipping her a few pieces of carrot that had been strategically concealed for just this moment. She was a fine horse and beautifully smooth with her dappled golden coat glistening in the summer sunshine.

He brushed her a little more and then softly ran his hand over her bulging girth. Checking her bag and the general conditions of her expectant state, he worked his way back to her head and patted her neck.

"There you go, old girl," he said softly. "It won't be much longer before it's your turn too."

Slipping her another piece of carrot, he had to smile at the memories of his efforts to win Dolly over. She had been the toughest of them all, though she was always willing to do anything for Hannah.

He looked across the pasture and toward the house to see the object of their mutual affections lying on the swing, reading a book and eating a pear while swaying gently back and forth in short passes. The babies amused themselves severally and as a whole, generally trying to join forces in figuring out the next way to escape the established confines of the picket fence.

"The babies," he smiled to himself, were nearly two and well on their way to escaping the classification of babyhood altogether. They were becoming full-fledged "children."

"The children," he repeated to himself. "It's time to stop calling them babies, I suppose."

Watching them a minute longer, he slipped Dolly the last piece of carrot, gathered up his brushes, and started off across the pasture to join his little family in the shade. Seeing him approach, Meredith squealed with delight and, as if on cue, they all headed toward him.

Breaking into a jog, he debated whether he should avoid the confusion at the gate altogether and jump the fence. Thinking again, he decided that "the children" didn't need any more bright ideas to add to their list of conquering skills.

"All right, little ones," he chimed, "let's let Daddy in." They were clambering around his legs as Nathan searched for a diversion. "Andy, look at that beautiful butterfly, son. Is that your butterfly?"

"No, it's mine!" cried Meredith.

It worked. Merrie, not wanting anything to belong to anyone but herself, immediately turned and began chasing the butterfly to claim for her own. The others, figuring that if Meredith was chasing something then it must be worthwhile, quickly turned and started chasing after her.

"Hi, honey," Hannah began. "Are you done already?"

"Done enough," he mused as he approached. "Say, do you suppose there's any room on that swing for me?"

Hannah smiled, sitting up slightly as he took a seat. She then settled her head back into his lap, trying to find her place in the book once again.

"Dolly is close, Hannah. It shouldn't be long."

Putting the book back down, she glanced across the pasture at the mares until her eyes at last fell on Dolly.

"Yes, she is huge this time, isn't she? I still remember how that felt. They say once your baby is born you forget all about it, but I haven't. It probably won't be quite so traumatic next time though with only one baby instead of three."

Nathan blew out a long sigh and looked up into the branches of the tree. "Be it one more or three more, love, I'm glad it's Dolly and not us. I couldn't do that again, not now, probably not for years. Look at you, Hannah, the babies . . ." he caught himself, "the children, are nearly two now and you've finally gotten your figure back. You wouldn't want to go through the last two years again would you?"

"Oh, I don't know. I think the figure I used to have is gone forever. I don't think it could get much worse."

Nathan stopped the swing short and looked into his wife's face. "No, Hannah; I couldn't bear to see you go through that again."

"Our chances of having triplets again would be so obscure; Peter said it would be next to impossible."

"It could be our chances at having any more at all might be obscure," he added, "and I don't suppose it would matter either way. We have three strong, healthy children."

"We only have one boy."

Nathan laughed. "I wouldn't put you through that merely to have more boys. It really doesn't matter, and you know that it's not important to me at all."

She looked off across the pasture again. "It's such a perfect day; don't you think? So lovely," She sighed while watching the breezes ripple through the grass as the shadows from the clouds drifted across the fields.

"It is nice, and a mite cooler under the trees here."

"So when do you think Dolly will foal?" she asked, casually working the conversation back to babies.

"I don't know; my guess is any day. Her bag is full and she looks very ready."

"Did you hear Janette is expecting again?"

"Yes, last month. Two babies in less than a year," he mused in tones that were something less than approving. "It is too bad she couldn't find a husband who would have a little more respect for her."

Hannah was quiet. "It's God that grants life, Nathan. She and Gabriel both are so happy for it. The restaurant is going well and they have that big old fancy house now with so many rooms to fill up. I'm glad for them."

"I suppose. I wonder if this one will be as early as the last?" he persisted in his disapproval.

Hannah smiled, but otherwise chose to ignore the comment. "I saw Reverend Sanderson over at Davy's earlier. I guess he's making rounds today. I wonder how married life is treating him."

"He married the dressmaker, didn't he; last month or so?"

"Yes, Linda Bailey; only it was closer to six months ago."

"Well if he's making rounds as you say, our lane is the next in line after David's. I'm sure we'll find out."

She smiled to herself. Reverend Sanderson had mentioned at church that he would be by later in the week and she knew he had good news to bring. It was news that she hoped Nathan would hear joyfully, but she would wait until he broke it himself. It shouldn't be long, for she thought she saw him leaving David's house a few minutes earlier.

"The children are having a good time," she ventured as they swung gently back and forth, while the three little ones laughed, pulling grass out of the lawn and throwing it at each other in a scene that resembled something akin to the glee of bath time. "They've been fun, Nathan; don't you think? And life has become so peaceful now."

"Yes," he agreed, "and I, for one, am enjoying that peacefulness. I'm not ready to give it up yet."

"At least you don't have a giant harvest to contend with this year."

"That is a relief, isn't it? More time for home and family."

"Hello there." Their conversation was stopped short by the approaching minister.

"Reverend Sanderson," Nathan said, nearly jumping to his feet. "Hello; we didn't hear you coming."

"Yes," he laughed. "It did seem a rather cozy scene there."

"Come in; come in, quickly, before the children beat you to the gate."

Nathan picked up Andrew, who happened to be in the lead, knowing that Meredith would instantly vie for the position. She would want to be held only seconds before struggling to be let down. For now, however, it created the perfect diversion to allow their visitor through the gate.

Once inside, Reverend Sanderson shook Nathan's hand and said hello to Hannah with, what Nathan perceived as, a definite gleam in his eye. He wondered at it only for a moment before dismissing it entirely. They would always be special friends, he supposed to himself; he knew he needn't be concerned.

"You have a wonderful family, Nathan," he said at last. "You must be pleased to have three such beautiful children."

"I am," he agreed. "They can be a handful at times, but we are very grateful for each of them. How is married life treating you, Reverend, and how is your wife?"

"Fine, fine, we are doing just fine and Linda is feeling much better now."

"Has she been sick?" he asked unsuspectingly.

"Just the usual," he laughed, "or so I suppose from what I hear. I'm afraid I've never been through this before. My first wife and I were never able to have children. This is a new experience for us both."

"Is she expecting then?" Nathan asked in surprise.

"Why, yes; didn't Hannah tell you?"

"I thought I'd let you break the good news, Carlen," she added, smiling to herself and pretending to watch the children across the yard as a diversion to meeting Nathan's glances.

"We're quite thrilled over the prospects. Tell me, Nathan, what was it like for you, becoming a father? Was it as exciting as it seems?"

"It was an experience," he agreed, thinking back to the moment. "There we were, just us, Hannah and I, and then within moments, Peter held up the first little girl. Suddenly, we were parents; we had a daughter." He chuckled to himself. "And then a few minutes later we had two daughters and, finally, after we thought we were all done and it was over, we had a son to boot." Nathan shook his head and sighed. "I'll never forget it; it was an inspiring moment. I hope it goes well for you both."

"I'm sure it will. Your mares are looking very fine. You're getting quite a herd out there."

"Ah yes," Nathan agreed, with a tone of certain satisfaction to his voice. "They are fine horses. I think I've looked forward to this day for half of my life."

"Well, it's nice to see people's dreams come true," the reverend agreed. "I'm glad you're all doing so well."

"How is everyone at my brother's house?" Hannah asked. "You were just there, weren't you?"

"Yes," Carlen smiled broadly. "Laurel was full of questions," he added with a laugh and a friendly little wink.

Hannah knew enough to let the subject drop completely, but Nathan, unbeguiled and unsuspecting, did not.

"What sort of questions?" he asked.

Changing his attentions, Carlen suddenly became a little more sober. "Oh, well . . ." he stammered, "it seems that while we were visiting, she suddenly remembered my name from a past conversation."

"With whom?" Nathan asked, while Hannah's head shot up, her eyes fixed on Carlen's own.

"What did you tell her?" Hannah asked, circumventing the response to her husband.

Carlen smiled calmly. "I told her the truth, of course."

"Oh," Hannah replied, looking off across the yard. "I guess I did sort of wonder if she'd ever put it all together."

Carlen laughed aloud. "Well, yes. I think it would be safe to assume that she has now."

"Mapleton?" Nathan guessed.

"Yes," the reverend answered.

"You know, I've always wondered just how serious the two of you were."

Hannah buried her face in her hands, while Carlen smiled at the action. "Surely, Hannah has told you everything," he answered.

"On the contrary," Nathan countered. "I think most of what I know, I've heard from you."

Carlen looked down at his feet, suddenly unsure of what to say.

"You said you would've married her," Nathan prompted, not wanting to let the moment pass.

"That I did," Carlen confessed. "Due to her age, I fought the temptation to out and out ask her nearly every time I was with her."

Hannah didn't say anything, but Carlen saw her lips curve into a smile, he assumed at the memories, while she looked at the book in her lap.

"What about you, Hannah?" Nathan persisted, taking full advantage of having them both present to finally satisfy his lingering curiosities.

"Oh, don't be mean, Nathan."

"Not at all, love; I'm merely curious."

"Obviously, God had his hand in the orchestration of . . ." Carlen was graciously trying to spare her the answer, but Nathan held up his hand to stop him.

"I trust you both completely, Reverend," he assured him, "but Hannah will never speak of it."

"Fine, Nathan!" she sighed in defeat. "I would have married him in an instant. You know me well enough to know that much. Then, I would have been the deceased first wife and you would be having some other conversation with Carlen today, while Cathleen Jackson sat on this swing with you."

"I could have never married Cathleen Jackson," he protested, though this time it was Hannah who held up her hand to stop him.

"As our good reverend has stated," she concluded, "God had his hand in the orchestration of the entire plan and I'm quite pleased with the results."

"Amen!" Carlen laughed.

Nathan looked at them both, before laughing himself. Yes, they would always be special friends.

Some further chitchat ensued between Carlen and Nathan concerning the weather and crops and the congregation, before the minister, at last having his fill of amusing interrogation for one day, announced it was time to be on his way.

"Congratulations, Reverend." Nathan stood and waved a final farewell. "Say hello to your wife, and come again."

Settling back into the swing, they watched the minister walk down the drive and then looked out across the pasture once more.

"They are fine horses," Hannah added in agreement. "But doesn't seeing all those little foals out there give you stirrings, at least a little, to have another baby?"

"Horses? No, not in the least."

Sighing she looked off a little despondently to the children across the yard, trying to figure out another approach.

"Did you know Alannah is expecting? Peter is so excited. They have Maggie of course, but for him this is a first and he . . ."

"Hannah," he interrupted, "I know what you're getting at and the answer is no, absolutely not."

"But Nathan . . ."

"No, Hannah. What if it was triplets again, or even twins? Don't you remember what you went through? Don't you remember how hard it was? I couldn't put you through that again. I'm sorry, Hannah, but no."

"You couldn't put me through it, or couldn't endure it yourself?" she asked.

He looked into her eyes and shook his head before he spoke again. "Neither." Then, as though the first time hadn't been definite enough, he repeated his stance. "The answer is no, Hannah, absolutely, unequivocally, no. We are barely recovering from the first ones. Surely, you remember how desperate we were for sleep and how difficult it all was. Don't you remember it at all?"

"Yes, of course I remember; but that was three babies and they're nearly two years old now. We made it all right."

"Well, I think I should have some say in the matter, and I say no."

There was a long moment of silence between them before she spoke quietly.

"And what if God says yes?"

Nathan smiled to himself. "He does seem to have had quite a bit to say about that today," he laughed. "But as to the matter in our family, I haven't heard God say one word about it, my love. Since he hasn't spoken to me, then I still have a say, and that would be no."

She was quiet a minute more, trying to think of a last approach, since all she had tried so far wasn't working.

"Don't you like children, Nathan?"

This time he out and out laughed. "I love children, and maybe three or four years in the future, maybe then we can think about having another; but not right now. I really have no desire for it."

"What about my desires? Do my desires count at all?"

He looked at her long enough to see a clear disappointment in her eyes before he looked off at the children, out at the horses and then over to the crops.

"Can we talk about something else?" he asked at last.

"What if it was only one?" she persisted.

"We couldn't guarantee it. Now, please, let's talk about something else."

She was very quietly staring off at nothing in particular and choosing not to say anything at all, wondering if she should go back to reading her book, when Nathan looked up to see Peter coming down the lane. Secretly, he was thankful for the diversion, hoping it would change the topic once and for all.

"Look, Hannah; it's Peter. I wonder what he's looking for out here."

Peter pulled to a stop, set the brake and jumped down from the carriage, barely making it through the gate before the children reached him.

"You have to be quick around here, I see. Hi, Nathan; how are you feeling, Hannah?" Hannah paled at the question, though Nathan didn't notice.

"How is Alannah feeling?" he added back.

"Oh, fine; she's really doing well, and Mother is looking so forward to having a couple more grandchildren."

"Couple?" Nathan questioned. "Is Alannah having twins?"

"As if you didn't know," Peter laughed, while Hannah buried her face deep in her hands and Nathan stared at his brother in perfect bewilderment.

"Why, no, Peter; I had no idea she was expecting twins."

Seeing the sincerity in his face and then noticing Hannah covering hers, Peter stopped mid-laugh and nervously cleared his throat.

"Uh, actually, she's not. It appears to be only one. I was referring to an addition into one of our other Layne families, but I think I might have spoken out of turn. It sounds as if maybe you haven't heard yet."

"No," said Nathan, "who is it?"

Hannah stood up, looking completely ill. "I think it has gotten past nap time. Nathan, can you help me get the children down?"

"Don't be silly, love; they're fine and happy. They can play while we visit."

Not knowing whether to faint or run, she sank back into the swing as Peter tried nervously to think of a way out of the predicament he had just caused.

"I'm sorry," he said at last. "I guess I spoke out of turn. Maybe we should change the subject."

"All right," he shrugged, "only now I wonder who it is. Though I'm glad it isn't us. Whoever it is, I'm thankful it is them and not us. It seems that 'God' is passing out babies to half of Silver Falls lately, and I'm glad for them. May they all have health and happiness, so long as it doesn't spread this direction."

"I've never known you to be so adamant about this sort of thing. I thought you loved children," Peter began, though Hannah stopped him.

"Nathan and I were just discussing the 'possibilities' before you came," she added weakly.

"Yes, and I don't mind letting it be known that my answer is no," he put in.

"Oh, I see," said Peter, rubbing his chin and trying to collect his thoughts. "Well, I'm quite thrilled myself that we've been fortunate enough to gain such a blessing. Can you imagine, Nathan? I'm going to be a dad at last."

"I'm thrilled for you, Pete. I'm sure you will love it."

Peter nodded and then glanced again at Hannah with a look that clearly said. "Did he really say no?"

"How is Maggie doing?" Hannah asked, hopeful of changing the subject.

"Splendidly!" Peter answered. "She appears to have fully adjusted to her new life. She is catching up to where she should be in size and development, and she has taken completely to Mother. Having her there feels so right to us all, as though she was always meant to be a natural part of our family."

"How old is she now?" Nathan asked, while Hannah offered a sigh of relief that his attentions had finally changed for good.

"She turned two last month. She is a couple months older than the triplets, though they are all quite a bit larger than she."

"I guess that accounts for them getting on as well as they do," Nathan mused.

"I suppose it does. Well," Peter concluded, "I should be on my way, but before I do, we were wondering if you would join us for dinner tomorrow night? Our house, at about six; Mother said she'd watch all the children if you did."

"We'd love to," Nathan answered. "What can we bring?"

"Just yourselves and your appetites; Alannah has it all planned out. I guess we'll see you then."

He was off, leaving them once again to their cozy afternoon in the swing. Only somehow, it wasn't quite as cozy as it had been for one of them. Nathan was speculating over which of his brothers' wives might possibly be expecting another child, while Hannah was feeling more ill by the moment.

"Hannah," he said at last, "do you know which family is having the other baby?"

"Yes," she offered honestly, though very quietly.

"Is it George's?"

"No Nathan. Not to my knowledge."

"John's?"

"No."

"Mark's?" he asked in a tone of complete astonishment.

Hannah merely shook her head.

"Then it's Caleb's. What's the big secret there?" he wondered. "If the cat's out of the bag, then it's out; they are clear in Colorado. Why would Peter feel so secretive about that?"

Swallowing hard she spoke tentatively. "Actually, I hadn't heard that they were."

Swinging back and forth a few more times, Nathan mentally went over each brother once again, trying in vain to think who he could have possibly missed.

"Well, surely, it wouldn't be Mother," he said, making Hannah laugh at the suggestion.

"No honey, it isn't Mother."

He grew quiet as they swung back and forth a few more times. Then, looking off toward the crops, he put his arm around his wife and drew her close.

"I suppose the harvest will be on us in the next few days."

"Yes," she agreed, "though it shouldn't be nearly as much work this year as in the past."

He nodded and then added. "The horses are doing well and the children are no longer babies, are they?"

"No, they are nearly two."

"Are you feeling well, Hannah?" he asked, kissing her forehead. "You look a little pale."

"I think I'm recovering," she offered.

Nathan looked up at the clouds in the sky. "Do you remember, love, when we used to lie in the meadow and imagine the shapes in the clouds? We were only children then, weren't we? I used to think up every excuse I could to be with you. I have always loved you." He held her close a little longer as a sheepish smile crept across his face.

"So, Hannah, my dear, I take it this means 'God said yes'?"

Tears welled up in her eyes as she nodded and then looked away.

Nathan shook his head and laughed, and then he was quiet for a very long time. At last, smiling, he shook his head again.

"Hannah, I don't know how you can live with me when I am being such a beast as today. I hope you will forgive me."

"I had no idea you would feel this way. It was a surprise for me as well, but such a happy one."

"Well," he said, after another lengthy pause, "if heaven doesn't consider me too complete a fool after today to revoke the blessing, then I will have to say, in the end, that I will be happy and thankful too."

Kissing her and holding her tightly, he gazed off over the fields one last time. "Yes, Hannah, my love," he concluded, "surely, it will be wonderful enough."

THE END

About the Author

Rebecca Woods lives a quiet life in the Midwest, where she enjoys writing, horses, symphonies, and farming with her family.

Angels and Promises of Silver Falls is the second of five volumes in the award-winning Silver Falls series. For more information, you can view her author page at facebook.com/pages/rebecca-woods.

0 26575 59971 8